KU-431-631

THE AGE OF DOUBT

LENHAM LIBRARY
11 THE LIMES
LENHAM ME17 2PQ

LEN
11/14

- 9 MAR 2015   15 JUL 2019   - 9 JUN 2023

1 4 APR 2015
- 5 OCT 2015

2 2 SEP 2016   2 9 JUL 2019

3 0 MAY 2017   - 7 APR 2020

2 8 OCT 2017   1 0 NOV 2021

1 5 MAR 2018

1 0 MAY 2018   - 1

1 3 DEC 2018

Please return on or
You can renew onli
or by telephone 08

CUSTOMER SERVICE EXCELLENCE   Libra

C161010248

THE AGE OF DOUBT

Translated by Stephen Sartarelli

ANDREA CAMILLERI

LARGE PRINT

Oxford

Copyright © Sellerio Editore, 2008
Translation Copyright © Stephen Sartarelli, 2012

First published in Great Britain 2012
by
Mantle
An imprint of Pan Macmillan

Published in Large Print 2013 by ISIS Publishing Ltd.,
7 Centremead, Osney Mead, Oxford OX2 0ES
by arrangement with
Pan Macmillan
A division of Macmillan Publishers Limited

All rights reserved

The moral right of the author has been asserted

British Library Cataloguing in Publication Data
Camilleri, Andrea.
    The age of doubt.
    1. Montalbano, Salvo (Fictitious character)
    - - Fiction.
    2. Police - - Italy - - Sicily - - Fiction.
    3. Detective and mystery stories.
    4. Large type books.
    I. Title
    853.9'14–dc23

KENT
ARTS & LIBRARIES

ISBN 978–0–7531–9098–2 (hb)
ISBN 978–0–7531–9099–9 (pb)

Printed and bound in Great Britain by
T. J. International Ltd., Padstow, Cornwall

CHAPTER
ONE

He had just fallen asleep after a night worse than almost any other in his life, when a thunderclap as loud as a cannon fired two inches from his ear startled him awake. He sat up with a jolt, cursing the saints. Sleep seemed a distant memory, never to return. It was useless to remain in bed.

He got up, went over to the window, and looked outside. It was a textbook storm: sky painted uniformly black, bone-chilling lightning bolts, billows twelve feet high charging forward, shaking their great white manes. The surging sea had eaten up the beach, washing all the way up under the veranda. He glanced at his watch: not quite 6a.m.

He went into the kitchen, prepared a pot of coffee, and sat down, waiting for it to bubble up. Little by little, the dream he had just had began to resurface in his memory. What a tremendous pain in the arse. This had been happening to him for several years now. Why did he always have to remember every shitty little thing he happened to dream? As far as he knew, not everyone, upon waking up, dragged their dreams behind them. They simply opened their eyes, and everything that had happened to them during their sleep, good and bad, disappeared. But not him. And the worst of it was that these were problematic dreams. They raised a great many questions for most of which he had no answer. And in the end he would always get upset.

The previous evening he had gone to bed in good spirits. A week had gone by at the station with nothing of importance happening, and he'd decided to take advantage of the situation to surprise Livia and appear at her doorstep in Boccadasse unannounced. He had turned out the light, lain down in bed, and fallen asleep almost immediately. He'd started dreaming at once.

"Cat, I'm leaving for Boccadasse tonight," he'd said, walking into the station.

"I'm coming too!"

"No, you can't."

"Why?"

"Because!"

At this point Fazio cut in.

"I'm sorry, Chief, but you really can't go to Boccadasse."

"Why?"

Fazio looked a little apprehensive.

"Do you mean to tell me you've forgotten, Chief?"

"Forgotten what?"

"You died yesterday morning at exactly seven fifteen."

And he pulled a little piece of paper out of his pocket.

"You, Salvo Montalbano, son of —"

"Knock it off with the public records! Did I really die?! How did it happen?"

"You had a stroke."

"Where?"

"Here, at the station."

"When?"

"When you's talkin' witta c'mishner," Catarella chimed in.

Apparently that son of a bitch Bonetti-Alderighi had pissed him off so badly that . . .

"If you want to come and have a look . . ." said Fazio, "a mortuary chapel was set up in your office."

They'd pushed aside the mountains of paper on his desk and laid the open coffin there. He looked at himself. He didn't look dead. But he was immediately convinced that the corpse in the coffin was his.

"Have you informed Livia?"

"Yes," said Mimi Augello, coming up to him. Then he hugged him tightly and said, crying, "I'm so sorry."

And a sort of chorus kept repeating: "We're so sorry."

The chorus was made up of Bonetti-Alderighi, his cabinet chief Dr Lattes, Jacomuzzi, Burgio the headmaster, and two undertakers.

"Thanks," the inspector said.

Then Dr Pasquano came forward.

"How did I die?" Montalbano asked him.

Pasquano flew off the handle.

"What! Still giving me grief, even in death! Just wait for the post-mortem results!"

"But can't you just give me a rough summary?"

"It looks like a sudden, massive stroke, but there are a few things that don't —"

"Oh, no you don't!" the commissioner broke in. "Inspector Montalbano can't investigate his own death!"

"Why not?"

"It wouldn't be right. He's too personally involved. Anyway, the law makes no allowance for that sort of thing. I'm sorry. The case will be assigned to the new captain of the flying squad."

At this point Montalbano got worried and took Mimì aside.

"When is Livia coming?"

Mimì seemed uneasy.

"Well, she said . . ."

"She said what?"

Mimì stared at his shoes.

"She said she didn't know."

"Didn't know what?"

"Whether she could make it to the funeral."

He stormed out of the room, enraged, and ran into the courtyard, which was crowded with funeral wreaths and a waiting hearse. He pulled out his mobile phone.

"Hello, Livia? Salvo here."

"Hi, how are you? Oh, I'm sorry, I didn't mean . . ."

"What's this about you not knowing if you can make it to —"

"Salvo, listen. If you had lived, I would have done everything in my power to stay with you. I might even have married you. After wasting my life chasing after you, what else could I do? But now that I'm suddenly faced with this unique opportunity, you must understand —"

He turned the phone off and went back inside. He noticed they'd put the lid back on the coffin and the cortège was starting to move.

"Are you coming?" Bonetti-Alderighi asked him.

"Yes, I suppose so," he replied.

But as soon as they got to the courtyard, one of the pallbearers fell, and the coffin crashed to the ground with a bang that woke him up.

After that, he'd been unable to fall asleep again, besieged by unanswered questions. One, above all, hammered away at him. What did Livia mean when she said she wanted to take advantage of the opportunity? Quite simply, it meant that his death represented a sort of liberation for her. The follow-up question could only be: how much truth was there in a dream? In this particular case, even a tiny grain of truth was too much. Because it was true that Livia had had more than her fill. In fact, she'd had enough to fill a whole boatload of shipping containers. But how was it possible that his conscience only showed up in dreams, ruining his sleep? All the same, he thought, the fact that Livia had no intention of coming down to Sicily for his funeral was not right, whatever her reasons might be. In fact, it was downright mean.

When he got into the car to go to the station, he noticed that the sea had come almost all the way up to the house and was less than a couple of feet from the parking area. He'd never seen the water come up this far. The beach was gone. It was all one great expanse of water.

It took him a good fifteen minutes and a couple of hundred curses before the car's engine decided to do

5

what it was supposed to do, and this, naturally, only aggravated the state of his nervous system, which was already on the ropes from the nasty weather conditions.

He'd gone barely fifty yards when he had to stop. There was a line of traffic extending as far as the eye could see — or, rather, as far as the windscreen wipers, which couldn't quite manage to wipe away the pouring rain, allowed the eye to see.

The column of traffic was made up entirely of cars headed towards Vigàta. In the opposite lane there wasn't so much as a moped.

After about ten minutes of this, he decided to pull out of the jam, turn back, and, at the junction with the Montereale road, take another route into town. It was longer, but it would at least get him to his destination.

But he was unable to budge, as the nose of his car was wedged right into the back of the car in front of him, and the car behind him had done the same to him.

It was hopeless. He had to stay put. He was trapped. Sandwiched. And the worst of it was that he had no idea what the hell had happened to create this situation.

After another twenty minutes or so he lost patience, opened the car door, and got out. In the twinkling of an eye he was soaked straight down to his underpants. He started running towards the front of the line of cars and soon came to the point of obstruction, the cause of which was immediately obvious: the sea had washed the road away. Completely. Both lanes were gone. In their place was a chasm, at the bottom of which lay not earth but foaming yellow water. The nose of the first car in the column was actually sticking out over the edge. Another ten inches and it would have plummeted down. The inspector, however, was immediately convinced that it was in danger, because the road surface was still crumbling, though very slowly. In twenty minutes, it was destined to be swallowed up in the chasm. The downpour made it impossible to see inside.

He went up to the car and tapped on the window. After a pause it was opened barely a crack by a young woman just over thirty wearing spectacles with lenses as thick as the bottoms of bottles. She looked terrified.

She was alone in the car.

"You have to get out," he said to her.

"Why?"

"I'm afraid your car's going to get swallowed up if help doesn't arrive immediately."

She made a face like a child about to cry. "But where will I go?"

"Take whatever you need, and you can come in my car."

She just looked at him and said nothing. Montalbano realized she didn't trust him, a total stranger.

"Listen, I'm a police inspector."

Perhaps it was the way he said it, but the girl seemed convinced. She grabbed a sort of handbag and got out of the car. They started running side by side, then Montalbano made her get in his car.

Their clothes were so wet that when they sat down their weight made the water ooze out of her jeans and his trousers.

"I am Montalbano."

The girl eyed him, bringing her head closer.

"Ah, yes. Now I recognize you. I've seen you on TV."

She started sneezing and didn't stop. When she eventually finished, her eyes were watering. She removed her glasses, wiped her eyes, and put them back on.

"My name is Vanna. Vanna Digiulio."

"Looks like you're catching a cold."

"Of course."

"Listen, would you like to come to my house? I've got some dry clothes that belong to my fiancée. You could change into them and put these clothes out to dry."

"I'm not sure that would be right," she objected, suddenly reserved.

"What?"

"That I come to your house."

What was she imagining? That he would jump on her the moment she entered? Did he give the impression of being that kind of man? And hadn't she ever looked at herself in the mirror?

"Listen, if you're not —"

"And how would we get to your house?"

"On foot. It's barely fifty yards from here. It will be hours before anyone gets us out of this jam."

As Montalbano, after changing clothes, prepared a latte for her and a bowl of coffee for himself, Vanna had a shower, put on a dress of Livia's that was a bit loose on her, and came into the kitchen, crashing first into the doorjamb and then against a chair. How did she ever get a driver's licence, with eyes like hers? A rather plain girl, poor thing. When she was wearing jeans, one

8

couldn't tell, but now that she was wearing Livia's dress, Montalbano noticed that she had bandy, muscular legs. They looked more like a man's legs than a woman's. And on top of almost non-existent breasts and a mousy face, she even had an ungainly walk.

"Where'd you put your clothes?"

"I saw a little heater in the bathroom, and I turned it on and put my jeans, blouse, and jacket in front of it."

He sat her down and served her the latte with a few of the biscotti Adelina normally bought for him and which he normally never ate.

"Excuse me a minute," he said after drinking his first cup of coffee, and he got up and phoned the station.

"Ah, Chief, Chief! Ahh, Chief!"

"What's wrong, Cat?"

"Iss the oppocalypso!"

"What happened?"

"The wind blew the roof tiles offa the roof in probable cause o' which the water's comin' inna rooms!"

"Has it done any damage?"

"Yessir. F'rinstince, alla papers that was a toppa yer desk awaitin' f'yiz to sign 'em 'sgot so wet they's turn to paste."

A hymn of exultation, deriding the bureaucracy, welled up joyously in Montalbano's breast.

"Listen, Cat, I'm at home. The road into town has collapsed."

"So you's consiquintly outta reach."

"Unless Gallo can find a way to come and get me . . ."

"Wait a sic an' I'll put 'im on, 'e's right here."

9

"What is it, Chief?"

"Well, I was on my way to the station when I ran into a traffic jam about fifty yards down the road from my house. The storm has washed away the road. My car is stuck there and I can't move it. And so I'm stranded at home. If you could manage to find a —"

Gallo didn't let him finish.

"I'll be there in half an hour, max," he said.

The inspector returned to the kitchen, sat down again, and lit a cigarette.

"Do you smoke?"

"Yes, but my cigarettes are all wet."

"Take one of mine."

She accepted and held out her cigarette for him to light.

"I feel mortified for causing you so much trouble —"

"Not at all! In half an hour somebody's going to come and pick me up. Were you on your way to Vigàta?"

"Yes. I had an appointment at ten, at the harbour. My aunt is supposed to be arriving. I came all the way from Palermo. But I doubt that in this weather . . . I bet she doesn't berth until this afternoon."

"There aren't any mail boats or ferries that come into the port at ten in the morning, you know."

"I know. My aunt has her own boat."

The word "boat" got on his nerves. Nowadays when someone says "come and see my boat", you find yourself looking at a ship of a hundred and twenty feet.

"Rowing boat?" he asked, innocent as a lamb.

She didn't get the joke.

"She's a big boat with a captain and a four-man crew. And she's always sailing. Alone. I haven't seen her for years."

"Where's she going?"

"Nowhere."

"I don't understand."

"My aunt likes sailing the high seas. She can afford it. Apparently she's very rich. When Uncle Arturo died, he left her a large inheritance and a Tunisian manservant named Zizì."

"So she bought the boat with her inheritance?"

"No, Uncle Arturo already had the boat. He also liked to spend a lot of time at sea. He didn't work, but he had a lot of money. Nobody knew where it came from. Apparently he had some sort of partnership with a banker named Ricca."

"And what do you do, if you don't mind my asking?"

"Me?"

She seemed to hesitate for a moment, as if she needed to choose from the many different things she did.

"I'm a student."

In the half-hour that followed, Montalbano learned that the girl, who was an orphan and lived in Palermo, was studying architecture, didn't have a boyfriend, and, well aware that she was no beauty, loved to read and listen to music. He also learned that she didn't use perfume, lived with a cat named Eleuterio in an apartment that she owned, and preferred going to the movies to sitting in front of the television. Then she stopped all at once, looked at the inspector, and said:

"Thanks."

"For what?"

"For listening to me. It's not every day that a man will sit and listen to me for so long."

Montalbano felt a little sorry for her.

Then Gallo arrived.

"The road's still out," he said, "but the firemen and road crews are at the site. It's going to take hours."

She stood up.

"I'm going to change."

When they went outside, the downpour had actually intensified. Gallo took the Montereale road, at the crossroads turned towards Montelusa, and a good half-hour later, they arrived in Vigàta.

"Let's take the young lady to the Harbour Office," the inspector said.

When Gallo pulled up, Montalbano said to Vanna:

"Go and see if they have any news. We'll wait for you here."

Vanna returned about ten minutes later.

"They said my aunt's boat sent word that they're proceeding slowly but are all right, and they expect to be in the harbour around four o'clock this afternoon."

"So what are you going to do?"

"What am I supposed to do? I'll wait."

"Where?"

"Oh, I dunno, I'm unfamiliar with this town. I'll go and sit in a cafe."

"Why don't you come with us to the police station? You'll be a lot more comfortable than in a cafe."

★　★　★

There was a small waiting room at the station. Montalbano sat her down there, and since he had bought a novel just the day before, *The Solitude of Prime Numbers*, he brought the book to her.

"Fantastic!" said Vanna. "I've been wanting to buy this. I've heard a lot of good things about it."

"If you need anything, ask Catarella, the switchboard operator."

"Thanks. You're truly a . . ."

"What's the name of your aunt's boat?"

"Same as mine. The *Vanna*."

Before leaving the room, he eyed the girl. She looked like a wet dog. The clothes she had put back on hadn't completely dried and were all wrinkled. Her bun of black hair had come apart and covered half her face. And she had a strange way of sitting that the inspector had noticed in certain refugees, who always look ready to leave the chair in which they are sitting, or to stay seated in that chair for eternity.

He stopped at Catarella's post. "Call the Harbour Office and tell them that if the *Vanna* contacts them again, I want to know what it said."

Catarella looked flummoxed.

"What's wrong?" the inspector asked.

"How's Havana gonna contact the Harbour Office?"

Montalbano's heart sank.

"Never mind. I'll do it myself."

CHAPTER
TWO

His office was unusable. Water was pouring from the ceiling as if there were ten broken pipes overhead. Since Mimì Augello wouldn't be coming in that morning, the inspector took over his deputy's room.

Around one o'clock, as he was getting up to go out for lunch, the phone rang.

"Chief, 'at'd be the Harbour Office onna phone, but I don' tink the man's a officer 'cause 'e says 'e's Lieutinnint wha'ss 'is name . . . damn, I forgot!"

"Cat, a lieutenant is an officer, even though you don't have to be an officer to work at the Harbour Office."

"Oh, rilly? So wha'ss it mean?"

"What's what mean? Never mind, I'll explain later. Put him on."

"Good afternoon, Inspector. This is Lieutenant Garrufo from the Harbour Office."

"Good afternoon. What can I do for you?"

"We've just had some news from the *Vanna*. They're not far offshore, in the waters just a short way beyond the port. But as the weather's not letting up, they think they won't be able to berth until about five o'clock,

14

since they'll have to sail a bit further out and take a different course, which —"

"Thanks."

"They said something else, too."

"And what was that?"

"Well, there was a lot of static on the line and I'm not sure we heard correctly, but there seems to be a dead man on board."

"One of the crew?"

"No, no. They'd just picked him up when they called us. He was in a dinghy that by some miracle hadn't sunk."

"Maybe from a shipwreck."

"Apparently not, as far as we could gather . . . But we'd better wait till they come into port, don't you think?"

He certainly did think they should wait.

He was almost certain, however, and would have bet his life on it, that the dead body belonged to some luckless, hungry, thirsty wretch who'd been waiting for weeks of hopeless agony to see the smoke of a steamship or even the simple outline of a fishing boat.

Better not think about such things, as the stories the fishermen told were horrific. The nets they cast into the water often came back up with corpses and body parts which they would throw back into the sea. The remains of hundreds and hundreds of men, women, and children who, after a ghastly journey through godforsaken deserts and wastelands that had decimated

15

their numbers, had hoped to come ashore in a country where they might be able to earn a crust of bread.

And for that journey they had given up everything, sold their bodies and souls, to pay in advance the slave traders who trafficked in human bodies and often did not hesitate to let them die, throwing them into the sea at the slightest sign of danger.

And then, for those survivors who made it to dry land, what a fine welcome they received in our country!

"Reception camps" they were called, though most often they were veritable concentration camps.

And there were even people — known, curiously, as "honourables" — who still weren't satisfied and wanted to see them dead. They said our sailors should shell their boats, since their human cargo were all disease-carrying criminals who had no desire to work.

Pretty much the same thing that had happened to our own people, way back when they left for America.

Except that now everyone had forgotten this.

When he thought about it, Montalbano was more than certain that, with the Cozzi-Pini law and similar bullshit, the Virgin Mary and Saint Joseph themselves would have never even made it to their cave.

He went to tell the girl about the phone call.

"Listen, the *Vanna* called the Harbour Office and said they'll be coming into port around five o'clock."

"Oh, well. I guess I'll have to sit tight. Can I stay here?"

She had accompanied her request with a hopeful hand gesture, like someone begging for alms.

"Of course you can," said the inspector. He couldn't very well kick a wet dog out of a temporary shelter.

Her smile of thanks made him feel so sorry for her that he asked without thinking:

"Actually, would you like to join me for lunch?"

Vanna immediately accepted. Gallo drove them to the restaurant, since it was still raining, though not quite as hard as before.

It was a pleasure to watch her eat. She set to her food as if she had been fasting for days. The inspector did not mention the corpse the *Vanna* had taken on board. It would have ruined her appreciation of the crispy fried mullets she was wolfing down with visible delight.

When they came out of the trattoria it had stopped raining. Glancing up at the sky, the inspector became convinced it wasn't just a momentary let-up, but that the weather was changing in earnest. There was no need to phone Gallo to come and pick them up. They returned to the station on foot, even though the road was more mud and water than asphalt.

The moment they got there, they found Gallo waiting for them.

"They've built a temporary bridge. You have to get your cars out of there at once."

It took them about an hour, but at last Vanna and Montalbano were able to drive back to Vigàta, each in their own car.

"Ahh, Chief! The Harbour's Office juss called sayin' as how the *Havana*'s comin' in to portside!"

Montalbano glanced at his watch. It was four-thirty.

"Do you know how to get to the port?" he asked Vanna.

"Yes, don't worry. I really want to thank you for your exquisite kindness, Inspector."

She took the novel out of her handbag and handed it to him.

"Did you finish it?"

"I've got about ten pages to go."

"Then keep it."

"Thanks."

She held her hand out to him, and he shook it. She stood there a moment, looking at him, then leapt forward, threw her arms around his neck, and kissed him.

It had stopped raining outside, but not in Montalbano's office. Water was still dripping from the ceiling. Apparently the space under the roof had become a leaking cistern. The inspector set himself up again in Augello's office. A short while later, there was a knock at the door. It was Fazio.

"The masons will be here tomorrow to fix the roof. The cleaning women will also be coming. I had a look at the papers that were on your desk. Might as well throw them away."

"So throw them away."

"And then what'll we do, Chief?"

"About what?"

"They all needed replies, but now we don't know what the questions were."

"What the hell do you care?"

"I don't. But what are you going to say to the commissioner when he starts asking you why you have so many outstanding memos unanswered?"

He was right.

"Listen, are any of them still intact?"

"Yes, sir."

"How many?"

"About thirty."

"Take them and put them under a tap. Let the water run over them for about two hours."

"But that'll ruin them, Chief!"

"That's the idea. When they're nice and soaked, put them with the already useless ones. We don't want to miss this excellent opportunity."

"But —"

"Wait, I haven't finished. Then take a chair, climb up on top of the filing cabinet, and pour about twenty jugs full of water over it. But without opening the drawers."

"So it'll look like the water came from the roof?"

"Exactly."

"Chief, the filing cabinet is made of iron. It's watertight."

Montalbano seemed disappointed.

"Oh, well. Forget about the cabinet."

Fazio looked bewildered.

"But why?"

"Look, before they can work out which documents were destroyed and redraft them, a good month, at the very least, will go by. Don't you think that's an incredible stroke of luck? A month without having to sign papers that are as useless as they are overdue?"

19

"If you say so . . ." said Fazio, leaving.

"Cat, call Dr Lattes for me."

He would tell the cabinet chief that they were forced to use boats to make their way around the station and that all their documents had become illegible. And he would also confess to a fear he had. Might this deluge not be the sign of an imminent Great Flood? For a bureaucrat and religious fanatic such as Lattes, such words might trigger a heart attack.

"Scuse me, Chief, but izzit possible fer summon a have a lass name of 'Garruso'?"

"No, I don't think so."

"But there's a liutinnint atta Harbour's Office onna phone who says 'ass 'is name, Garruso. Mebbe 'e's from up north."

"Why do you say that?"

"Cuz 'ss possible the Northers don' know iss a bad word down 'ere, Chief."

"No need to worry, Cat. The lieutenant's name is 'Garrufo', with an f."

"Jeez, whatta rilief!"

"Why do you care so much?"

"Well, I's a li'l imbarissed to call a liutinnint a 'garruso'."

"Put him on."

"Inspector Montalbano? This is Garrufo."

"What can I do for you, Lieutenant?"

"We've got a problem. The dead man."

People often say that death is a liberation. For those who die, naturally. Because for those who go on living it's almost always a colossal pain in the arse.

"Explain."

"Dr Raccuglia is on the scene here, and he very strongly advised that we ask you to come and have a look."

Raccuglia was the Harbour physician, a serious, much-admired person. On top of that, the inspector liked him. And so he really had no choice but to go and have a look, as the lieutenant put it.

"All right, I'm on my way."

As soon as he stepped outside he noticed that the sky was perfectly clear again. Only the gleaming constellation of puddles in the street bore witness to what had happened just a few hours before. The sun was beginning to set, but was strong enough to make it hot outside. Sicily's getting to be like a tropical island, the inspector thought, with rain and sunshine continually alternating in a single day. Except that, according to what one saw in 'Murcan films, on tropical islands you could eat, drink, and not give a fuck about anything, whereas here you only ate what the doctor allowed you to eat, drank only what your liver allowed you to drink, and every minute of life was a kick in the groin. That made quite a difference.

The so-called boat was a rather large and elegant yacht, and it was berthed at the central quay. It was flying, who knew why, the Panamanian flag. Waiting for him at the foot of the ladder was a naval lieutenant, who must have been Garrufo, and Dr Raccuglia.

A short distance away, a sailor from the Harbour Office stood guard over a dinghy lying on the quay.

There was no sign of anybody on the yacht's decks. The owner and crew must have been below.

"What's the problem, Doctor?"

"Sorry to make you come all the way here, but I wanted you to see the body before the ambulance comes and takes it away to Montelusa for the post-mortem."

"Why?"

"Because the corpse shows certain —"

"I'm sorry, Doctor, I didn't make myself clear. Why do you think the matter falls within my jurisdiction? Wasn't the body found in international —"

"The dinghy with the corpse in it," Lieutenant Garrufo interrupted him, "was intercepted just outside the mouth of the harbour, not in international waters."

"Oh," said Montalbano.

He'd tried to unload the case onto someone else and it hadn't worked. But perhaps all was not lost, and he could still push the bitter cup away from his lips. (Damn clichés!)

"But the boat may have been brought here from far away by the currents, which have been very strong with all the bad weather . . ."

Garrufo smiled at this second, pathetic attempt.

"Inspector, I realize it's a headache for you, but there's no doubt whatsoever that the boat had just drifted out of this port, indeed because of the very same currents you mention. Understand?"

The lieutenant placed special emphasis on the last word. Montalbano surrendered.

"All right, let's have a look," he said. "Where is he?"

"Follow me," said the lieutenant. "I'll lead the way."

On deck, not a soul. They went below to the mess room. On the table in the middle of the space lay the body, covered by an oilcloth.

Montalbano had imagined the corpse differently. Lying before him was a well-built male specimen of about forty, completely naked. Aside from the face, there were no wounds or scars on the front of the body. The face, on the other hand, had been reduced to a pulp of flesh and bone that didn't look like anything.

"Did you take off his clothes or was he . . .?"

"They told me that's how they found him in the dinghy. Naked," said Garrufo.

"And on the back, are there any —?"

"No wounds on the back, either."

A sickly-sweet smell festered in the room. The corpse wasn't fresh. As the inspector was about to ask another question, a woman appeared through a door, dressed in greasy overalls and wiping her hands with an equally greasy rag.

"How much longer are you going to keep that thing here?" she asked gruffly.

She opened the door to one of the two cabins giving on to the mess room, went inside, and closed the door.

At once a man of about fifty with a goatee came in, skinny as a rail and sunburnt, wearing spotless, wrinkleless white trousers, a blue blazer with silver buttons, and a military sort of cap on his head.

"Hello. I'm Captain Sperli," he said, introducing himself to Montalbano.

Apparently he'd already met the other two. Based on his accent, he had to be from Genoa.

"Is your engineer a woman?" the inspector asked.

The captain chuckled.

"No, she's the owner. Since the auxiliary engine wasn't doing too well, which is what's been holding us up for so long, the lady wanted to check it out for herself."

"And she's competent?" Montalbano asked again.

"She certainly is," said the captain. Then, in a lower voice: "She's better than the engineer himself."

At that moment they heard someone calling from the deck.

"Anybody there?"

"I'll take care of this," said the captain.

A few moments later, two men in white tunics came down, lifted the oilcloth together with the corpse, and carried it away.

"In your opinion, Doctor," Montalbano said, "how long —"

He was interrupted by the reappearance of the captain. Behind him was a sailor in a black woollen sweater with the name *Vanna* written across the chest. In his hands he had a bottle of white spirit and a rag. He cleaned off the surface of the tabletop and then spread over it a white tablecloth he had taken from a small cupboard.

"Please make yourselves comfortable," said the captain. "Will you have a drink?"

Nobody declined.

"In your opinion, Doctor," Montalbano began again after a sip of a whisky he'd never had before and which tasted like the best he'd ever drunk, "how long —"

The cabin door opened again, and the woman reappeared. She had changed into jeans and a blouse. She had no trace of jewellery on her. She was tall, dark, attractive, and elegant. She must have been close to fifty but had the body of a forty-year-old. She went to the cupboard, took a glass, and held it out, without a word, in front of the captain. He filled it almost to the brim with whisky. Still standing, she brought it to her lips and drank half of it in a single gulp. Then she wiped her lips with the back of her hand and said to the captain:

"Sperlì, tomorrow morning we're getting out of here, so I want you to —"

"Just a minute," Montalbano cut in.

The woman looked at him as if noticing only then that he was there. And instead of speaking to him directly, she addressed the captain.

"Who's he?"

"He's Inspector Montalbano."

"Inspector of what?"

"Police," replied the captain, a bit embarrassed.

Only then, after looking him up and down, did the woman deign to ask him directly:

"What were you going to say?"

"There's no way you can leave the port tomorrow."

"And why not?"

"Because we have to investigate the circumstances of the man's death. The judge is going to want to question you and —"

"What did I say, Sperli?" the woman asked severely.

"All right, all right, just drop it," the captain said.

"Signora, tell me, too, what you said to the captain," Montalbano butted in.

"I'd simply advised him to forget about the dinghy and not bring the body on board because it was bound to create a host of problems for us. But he —"

"I am a man of the sea," said the captain, to justify his actions.

"You see, signora —" Lieutenant Garrufo began.

"No, I don't see, I've seen enough," the woman cut him off, upset. Then, setting her empty glass down on the table, she added: "And how long, Inspector, do you think we'll be kept here?"

"In the best case, no more than a week, signora."

She stuck her hands in her hair.

"But I'll go crazy! What the hell am I going to do in this hole?"

Despite her obnoxious words and manner, the woman was unable to make Montalbano dislike her.

"You can visit the Greek temples of Montelusa," he suggested, half seriously and half jokingly.

"And then what?"

"Then there's the museum."

"And then what?"

"I don't know, you could visit some of the neighbouring towns. In Fiacca, for example, they make a kind of pizza called *tabisca*, which has —"

"I'll need a car."

"Can't you use your niece's?"

She looked at him in amazement. "What niece?"

CHAPTER
THREE

Maybe she has more than one, the inspector thought.

"Your niece Vanna."

The woman looked at him as if he was speaking in tongues.

"Vanna?!"

"Yes, about thirty, with glasses and black hair, lives in Palermo, and her surname is . . . wait . . . ah, Digiulio."

"Ah, yes. She's already left," the woman replied abruptly.

Montalbano noticed that, before replying, she had exchanged a quick glance with the captain. But he realized this wasn't the time to press the matter.

"Perhaps you could rent a car, with or without a driver," Dr Raccuglia suggested.

"I'll think about it," she said. "And now, if you'll excuse me."

She withdrew into her cabin.

"Nice disposition," said the lieutenant.

Captain Sperlì rolled his eyes heavenward, as if to evoke all the things he had to put up with, then threw up his hands.

"I think you wanted to ask me something," the doctor said to the inspector.

"It's no longer important," Montalbano replied. He had other things to think about.

When they went back on deck, the inspector noticed that there was now a huge motorboat moored alongside the yacht, so big he'd only seen its equal in Bond movies. And, lo and behold, it was flying the Panamanian flag.

"Did that just come in?" he asked the lieutenant.

"No, that cruiser's been in the harbour for the past five days. It's here for an engine check. They realized it wasn't running properly and summoned a technician from Amsterdam."

Back on the quay, Montalbano read the cruiser's name: *Ace of Hearts*. Dr Raccuglia said goodbye to the two men and headed for his car.

"There's something I want to ask you," the lieutenant said to Montalbano.

"Go ahead."

"Why were you so interested in the *Vanna* even before they told us they'd found the dinghy with the corpse in it?"

Smart question, worthy of a cop, and it put the inspector in a bit of a quandary. He decided to sing only half the Mass to the lieutenant.

"The niece I mentioned, the one the lady said had just left, had turned to the police because . . ."

"I see," said Garrufo.

"I think you'll be hearing from me again very soon," Montalbano said to him.

"I'm at your service." They shook hands.

★ ★ ★

He followed the lieutenant's car for a short distance, waited for him to park, get out, and go into the Harbour Office, then waited five more minutes and did the same himself.

"Can I help you?" the guard asked him.

"I need some information on recruitment."

"First door on the right."

Behind a counter sat an old officer with the *Settimana Enigmistica* in his hand.

"Good afternoon. I'm Inspector Montalbano," said the inspector, showing the man his badge.

"What can I do for you?"

"Were you on duty here this morning?"

"Yes."

"Do you remember whether a young woman of about thirty with glasses came in here asking if you had any news of a yacht, the *Vanna*, which was —"

"Just a second," the officer interrupted him. "I remember the girl perfectly well, but she didn't ask me anything about a yacht."

"Are you sure?"

"Look, Inspector, you're the fourth person to come into this office all day. Three men, counting you, and one girl. How could I be mistaken?"

"And what did she ask you?"

"She asked me if there was a sailor who worked here at the Harbour Office named . . . Give me a minute to check, because I also asked the Coast Guard . . . Here it is, Angelo Spitaleri, a cousin of hers."

"And does he work here?"

"No."

That girl, whose real name might be anything at this point, had taken him for a nice little ride, no doubt about it.

A little wet dog, she had seemed to him! He'd even felt sorry for her!

Whereas in fact she must be a very great actress. He could only imagine how hard she must have laughed inside at this inspector she was able to manipulate like a puppet.

But what could be her reason for telling him such a pile of lies? She must have had a purpose. But what?

Despite the late hour, he returned to the station. Gallo was still there.

"Listen, do you remember the licence-plate number of the car belonging to the girl who spent the day here?"

"I didn't look, Chief. All I remember is that it was a blue Fiat Panda."

"So there's no way to identify her?"

"I'm afraid not, Chief."

The inspector called Catarella in.

"That girl from this morning . . ." he began.

"The one 'at was waitin' inna waitin' room?"

"That's the one. Did she come and talk to you at any point or ask you anything?"

"She come once, Chief."

"What did she want?"

"She wannit a know where there's a batroom."

"And did she go?"

"Yessir, Chief. I's 'er escort."

"Did she do anything strange?"

Catarella blushed.

"I dunno."

"What do you mean, you don't know? Did she or didn't she?"

"How's am I asposta know what the young lady did inna batroom? I 'eard 'er pull the chain, but —"

"I wasn't referring to what she did in the bathroom! I meant did she do anything strange when you were escorting her?"

"I don' remimber, Chief."

"All right, then, you can go."

"Unless you's referrin' to the noise."

"What noise?"

"Seein' as how the foresaid young lady was carryin' a kinda cloth bag in 'er hand, as the foresaid young lady was goin' in, the foresaid bag crashed aginst the door frame, producin' the foresaid noise."

Montalbano could barely refrain from getting up and pummelling him.

"And what kind of noise was it?"

"Like a kinda heavy, metal-like ting. An' so I axed m'self wha' coulda made the noise. An iron bar? A horseshoe? A li'l branze statue? A —"

"Could it have been a weapon?" the inspector cut in, interrupting the litany.

"A dagger?"

"Or a gun, a pistol."

Catarella thought this over for a minute.

"Possible."

"All right, go and get me the Palermo phone book."

It was something he had to do simply to set his mind at rest. He looked for Vanna Digiulio, thinking it would be useless, but then he actually found the name in the directory.

He dialled the number and a woman's voice answered, though it was quite different from the girl's voice.

"Hello, this is Dr Panzica, I was looking for Vanna."

"Vanna? Vanna Digiulio?"

What was so strange about that?

"That's right."

"But she died years ago!"

"I'm sorry, I didn't know."

"And who are you, may I ask?"

"Fabio Panzica, a notary. It was over a question of inheritance."

At the mere mention of the word inheritance, people almost always rush forward faster than a school of starved fish. And this case was no exception.

"Perhaps it would be better if you gave me a few more details," the woman said.

"Gladly. But who are you, if I may ask?"

"I am Matilde Mauro. I was Vanna's best friend, and she left me her apartment in her will."

And, sure as death, Mrs Mauro now was hoping for a supplement to that inheritance.

"May I ask, Mrs Mauro, how Vanna died?"

"On a mission. The helicopter she was in crashed. She was unharmed but immediately captured. Since they thought she was a spy, she was tortured and then killed."

Montalbano balked.

"But when was this? And where?"

"In Iraq. Two months before Nasiriya."

"Why was this never reported?"

"Well, it was a covert mission, as they say. I can't tell you any more than that."

And he didn't want to know any more, either. It was an interesting case but, as far as he was concerned, he was merely wasting his time.

"I thank you for your courtesy, signora, but . . . Do you by any chance know any other Vanna Digiulios?"

"No, I don't, I'm sorry."

Dining on the veranda was out of the question. True, half a day had gone by without more rain, but it was still too damp. He laid the table in the kitchen, but didn't feel much like eating. He was still smarting from being made a fool of by the girl. He sat down, took a pen and a sheet of paper, and started writing a letter to himself.

Dear Montalbano,

Glossing over the distinction of Idiot Emeritus that you earned by letting the so-called Vanna Digiulio (clearly an assumed name) lead you around by the nose, I feel I have no choice but to bring the following to your attention:

1) Your meeting with Vanna was pure chance. But as soon as she learned that the person taking her to safety was you, a well-known police inspector, she was able to exploit the situation with

great skill and lucidity. What does this mean? That Vanna is a person endowed with quick reflexes and a keen ability to adapt to unforeseen situations in order to gain maximum advantage from them. As for her humble, wet-dog manner, which touched you so deeply, that was just a put-on, not an amateur but a professional performance, staged to fool a sitting duck (rhymes with stupid fuck) like you.

2) There is no doubt that Vanna was aware of the imminent arrival of the *Vanna*.

3) There is no doubt that Vanna is not the niece of the yacht's owner.

4) There is no doubt, however, that she is, in some way, and for reasons unknown, known to the owner and to Captain Sperli (the glance they exchanged was rather telling).

5) There is no doubt that Vanna has never been on board the *Vanna*.

6) There is no doubt that by saying Vanna had left, and thereby ending all discussion of the subject, the yacht's owner wanted to avoid arousing suspicion in you, my dear inspector.

7) There is no doubt that, in having no doubts, you find yourself, without a doubt, neck-deep in shit.

So perhaps you'd better start thinking of some doubts you may have.

Come to think of it, when Vanna was drinking her latte, she told you some things about her supposed aunt that she had no reason whatsoever to tell you. But she said them anyway.

A few examples:

1) That the aunt's husband, Arturo, was very rich.

2) That he had bought the *Vanna* and left it to his wife in his will.

3) That he was always at sea (like his widow, after him).

4) That nobody knew how he had earned all the money he had. In other words, with this last statement, Vanna left the field open to every supposition, even the worst. Why did she want to instil such doubt in you? She could have avoided it. But she didn't.

Think about it. Affectionately yours,

Since it was still too early to go to bed, he sat down in the armchair and turned on the TV. On the Free Channel, his friend the newsman Nicolò Zito was interviewing a man of about fifty with a beard, who turned out to be Captain Zurlo, chief pilot of the port.

Naturally, they were talking about the topic of the day, the *Vanna*'s discovery of the stray dinghy. Zito's questions were, as always, quite intelligent.

"Captain Zurlo, how far from the harbour mouth did the people on the *Vanna* say they were when they spotted the dinghy?"

"A little more than an Italian mile."

"Why do you say 'Italian'? Aren't all miles the same?"

"Theoretically speaking, a nautical mile, being one sixtieth of one degree of a meridian, should correspond to 1,852 metres. But in fact, in Italy it is equal to 1,851 metres and 85 centimetres; in England it's 1,853 metres and 18 centimetres; in the US it's —"

"Why these differences?"

"To make life complicated."

"I know exactly what you mean. Therefore we can say that the dinghy with the corpse inside was very close to the port?"

"Quite so."

"Could you explain for us why the *Vanna*, after taking the dinghy and corpse on board, took so many hours to enter the port? Was it because of the storm?"

The captain smiled.

"It wasn't actually a storm, far from it."

"No? Then what was it?"

"Technically speaking, it's called a strong gale, corresponding to a wind of force nine on the Beaufort scale."

"In plain language?"

"It means that the wind is approaching forty-five knots and waves can reach a height of twenty feet. The *Vanna* was in danger of running against the eastern arm. Since the auxiliary engine wasn't working very well, they had to go back out to the open sea and find a more favourable position."

"How come the dinghy hadn't capsized?"

"Chance, or maybe it was balanced between two conflicting currents."

"Here comes the most important question. In your opinion, with your many years of experience, was the dinghy being carried away from the port by the currents, or was it heading towards the port, also on the currents?"

Montalbano pricked up his ears.

"It's rather hard to say with any certainty. You see, there's always a current flowing out of the port, but it's also true that, given the weather conditions, this permanent current was nullified, so to speak, by the stronger currents coming in from the south-east."

"But what's your personal opinion?"

"I wouldn't want to be held to this in an official report, but I'd say the dinghy was probably being carried by the outward current."

"So it had come from inside the harbour?"

"What do you mean by 'inside'?"

"The central quay, for example."

"No, if the dinghy had started there, it would have ended up against the eastern arm."

"So where did it come from, in your opinion?"

"Probably from a point much closer to the harbour mouth."

"Thank you very much, Captain."

As the inspector lay down in bed, something was troubling him, but it did not prevent him from getting a good night's sleep.

When he got to Vigàta just before nine o'clock the next morning, he didn't go straight to the station but pulled up in front of the Harbour Office.

"Can I help you?" asked the usual guard.

"I'd like to speak to Lieutenant Garrufo."

"Please ask at the information desk."

The officer at the counter looked as if he hadn't moved since the day before. He was in exactly the same position, holding the same issue of the *Settimana Enigmistica* in his hand. Maybe he never went home to sleep. Maybe in the evening a sailor came in and covered him with an oilcloth, turned off the light, and closed the door behind him. The following morning, the cleaning crew would wash the oilcloth, dust the man off, and he would go back to work.

"I'm looking for Lieutenant Garrufo."

"He's not in."

"Is there anyone here in his place?"

"Of course. Lieutenant Belladonna."

"I'd like to —"

"Just a minute. You, if I remember correctly, are Inspector Montalbano."

The man picked up the telephone, dialled a number, said a few words, and hung up.

"The lieutenant is waiting for you. Second floor, second door on the right."

The door was open and the inspector instinctively poked his head inside. He was sure it was the wrong room, and so he knocked on the next door down.

"Come in."

He opened the door and went in. The officer sitting behind the desk stood up. Montalbano realized he'd got the wrong room again. The man had the rank of captain.

"I was looking for Lieutenant Belladonna."

"It's the door before this one."

So he hadn't been mistaken after all. Lieutenant Belladonna was a woman.

"May I come in? I'm Inspector —"

"Please come in and sit down," she said, getting up to greet him.

The lieutenant not only lived up to her surname, she exceeded it. She wasn't just beautiful; she was a knockout. For a brief moment, Montalbano was speechless. She was a good six inches taller than him, dark, with bright, sparkling eyes, red lips in no need of lipstick, and, above all, a very pleasant manner.

"I'm entirely at your disposal," she said.

I wish! thought the inspector.

"I'm not sure if you're aware of the corpse that was found by the people on a yacht sailing —"

"I know the whole story."

"There's one thing I'd like to know. When a craft wants to call at our port, does it have to give you advance notice of its arrival?"

"Of course."

"And its time of arrival?"

"Especially."

"Why?"

"For any number of reasons: ships manoeuvring inside the harbour, lack of berths, availability of pilots . . ."

"I see. If it's not too much trouble for you, could you tell me how far in advance the *Vanna* notified you that it would be calling at port here?"

"Yes, I can. Come with me."

Following her, Montalbano was spellbound by the undulating motion her skirt made as she walked. They came to a vending machine.

"Would you like some coffee?"

"I'd love some."

Montalbano let her work the machine. He was utterly inept at such things. He always pushed the wrong buttons, and instead of coffee he got plastic-wrapped sandwiches, ice-cream cones, or sweets. The coffee was good.

"Please wait for me here," she said.

The lieutenant opened a door over which there was a sign saying AUTHORIZED PERSONNEL ONLY and went inside. She returned five minutes later.

"Actually, the *Vanna* wasn't expected," she said. "They contacted us at six o'clock yesterday morning, saying they were forced to head for our harbour because of the terrible weather conditions."

This was the confirmation he had wanted of the concern that had come into his mind before falling asleep. How did the girl who called herself Vanna know that the yacht was supposed to arrive that morning? She must have been informed very early that same morning. Had she received this information from someone at the Harbour Office, or from the yacht itself?

Montalbano thanked the woman and took his leave.

"I'll come downstairs with you," she said. "I'd like to have a cigarette outside."

They smoked their cigarettes together. She said her name was Laura. And since they hit it off well, they each smoked a second cigarette while telling each other a few things about themselves. When they said goodbye, it was clear that they would have liked to smoke another ten cigarettes together.

CHAPTER
FOUR

Getting out of the car, he saw two masons on the roof of the police station. As he watched them, he felt suddenly worried.

"Get me Fazio," he said to Catarella, going in.

His office had been cleaned, but the ceiling was covered with damp spots. Once they dried, they would have to be painted over. He also noticed with some satisfaction that there wasn't a single document to be signed on his desk.

"Good morning, Chief."

"Listen, Fazio, what sort of protection do these masons have? I wouldn't want our police station to contribute to the increase in work-related murders."

For years that's what he'd been calling them, murders, not work-related deaths, because he was more than convinced that ninety per cent of the fatal accidents were the fault of the work providers.

"Not to worry, Chief. They're wearing safety harnesses. You may not have noticed."

"So much the better. Fazio, I need you to do one of those things you're so good at."

"What?"

"I want you to go on board the *Vanna* — with the excuse, say, that you need to draw up a complete list of the people to be summoned by the prosecutor — and get me all the vital information you can, official and unofficial, on the owner of the boat, the captain, and the four crew members."

Fazio gave him a questioning look.

"I'm sorry, Chief, but what would any of that information have to do with the corpse they found?"

Good question, but dictated by the fact that Fazio knew nothing of what the inspector had discovered concerning the so-called niece, Vanna.

"I'm just curious."

Fazio looked even more doubtfully at him.

"And what do you plan to do with all this official and unofficial information?" he asked after a pause.

"I want to know what the mood is on that boat, what sort of relationships they have among themselves . . . You know, people who spend so much time together, in such a small space, morning, noon, and night, often end up hating each other or can't stand one another . . . Sometimes a word slips out and the whole house of cards collapses."

This explanation clearly failed to convince Fazio, but he didn't venture to ask anything else.

Towards late morning, the inspector decided to phone the medical examiner.

It was probably too early to do so, but there was no harm in trying.

"Montalbano here. I'm looking for Dr Pasquano."

"The doctor's busy," the operator said.

"Could you do me a favour?"

"If possible."

"Could you find out from his assistant when the doctor plans to perform the post-mortem on the body that was found at sea yesterday?"

"Just a minute."

By the time the other person came back, Montalbano had already reviewed the multiplication tables for seven and eight. It was a good way to make the time pass when he had to wait.

"He's working on it right now."

"I'm so sorry, Inspector," Enzo said, throwing his hands up the moment Montalbano walked into the trattoria.

"What are you sorry about?"

"I haven't got any fresh fish. With the bad weather yesterday . . ."

"What have you got?"

"An antipasto of caponata made by my wife, a first course of pasta *alla norma* or with broccoli, and then, as a second course, an aubergine *parmigiana* that'll have you licking your fingers."

He was right. But instead of licking his fingers or his moustache, the inspector decided to order a second helping of aubergine.

Once outside, he realized he needed to take a long meditative-digestive walk all the way out to the lighthouse at the end of the jetty. He'd really stuffed himself this time. He even decided to go a bit out of his way, so he could walk past the *Vanna* and the *Ace of Hearts* berthed beside it.

There wasn't anybody on the deck of either boat, which probably meant that they, too, were eating.

When he got to the end of the jetty, he sat down on the usual flat rock. The spot afforded him a good view of the yacht and cruiser.

Halfway through his cigarette, he noticed a wooden crate, of the sort used for fish, floating on the water near the *Ace of Hearts*. He remembered what the chief pilot, Zurlo, had said on TV, and decided to wait and see where the currents would take it.

Sticking a hand in his pocket, he counted the cigarettes he had left. There were about ten; that would suffice.

A good hour later, the crate got wedged against the breakwater protecting the arm of the jetty. Captain Zurlo had been right. The outward currents, starting from the quay, necessarily carried all floating objects as far as the eastern arm, exactly where he was sitting.

He had an idea.

Making his way over the rocks, slipping and cursing, he was able to recover the crate. Grabbing it, he brought it back to the flat rock, and then chucked it back into the sea.

This time, it took barely half an hour for him to see that the crate was heading straight out of the harbour.

He got back in his car and headed off to Montelusa to talk to Dr Pasquano.

"The doctor's in his office," said the operator/doorman.

Arriving at the door, Montalbano knocked. No answer.

He knocked again. Nothing. So he turned the knob and went in. Pasquano was sitting behind the desk, engrossed in writing, and didn't even look up to see who had come in. "I'll bet my balls," he said, "that it was the woefully impolite Inspector Montalbano who just entered the room."

"Your balls are safe, Doctor. You're right on the money."

"Only momentarily safe, because you certainly will now try to break them."

"Right again."

"If only I could be so right when I play poker!"

"How'd it go at the club last night?"

"Don't remind me! I had three-of-a-kind in my hand and asked for two cards and . . . Never mind. What do you want?"

"You know damn well what I want."

"Just over forty, athletic build, in perfect physical condition, white skin, no sign of surgery, teeth that had never seen a dentist, perfect heart and lungs, and he wore neither glasses nor contact lenses. Is that enough for you?"

"Yes, for when he was alive. And after his death?"

"Let's say that when he was found, he'd been dead for at least three days."

"Was he killed when they smashed up his face that way?"

"Nuh-unh," said the doctor, shaking his head.

"Shot or stabbed?"

"Nuh-unh."

"Strangled?"

"Nuh-unh."

"You could at least say if I'm getting warmer or colder! Eh? A little help, the way they do on quiz shows?"

"Poisoned, my friend."

"With what?"

"Common rat poison."

Montalbano was so obviously bewildered that Pasquano noticed. "Do you find that disturbing?"

"Yes. Nowadays, poison is —"

"No longer in fashion?"

"Well . . ."

"Listen, I would strongly advise all aspiring murderers to use it. A gunshot makes such a racket that the neighbours are sure to hear it; stabbing spatters blood all over the place: on the floor, the walls, your clothes . . . Whereas poison . . . Don't you agree?"

"And what about his face?"

"They worked on that post-mortem."

"Apparently to make it harder to identify him."

"I'm glad to see that, despite your considerably advanced age, you, Inspector, still possess a certain degree of lucidity."

Montalbano decided to ignore the provocation. "What state are the fingertips in?"

"Intact, in keeping with the rest of the body except the face."

"Which means his fingerprints are not on file."

"Impeccable conclusion, deduced by extreme logical rigour. Congratulations. And now, if you've finished turning my balls to dust . . ."

"One last question. Was he married?"

"You're asking me? All I know is that there was no trace of a ring on any of his fingers. But that means nothing."

"Another thing. Can you tell me —"

"Oh, no you don't, my friend! You said your question about his marital status was the last. Keep your word for once in your life!"

Since he was already in Montelusa, he went to central police headquarters, to see if he could talk to someone in Forensics. He knew that the chief of Forensics, Vanni Arquà, whom he couldn't stand, was on holiday, with his deputy Cusumano taking his place.

"What can you tell me?" Montalbano asked him.

"Where should I start?"

"The dinghy."

"A small dinghy —"

"Actually, were there oars? I didn't see any."

"No. They were either lost at sea or the boat was towed. To continue: a small dinghy made in England. There are quite a lot of them around. No fingerprints; whoever handled it used gloves at all times. And the body was put in it only a short time before the boat was found."

"Thanks."

"One more thing about the dinghy. It showed no sign of having been used before."

"Meaning?"

"Meaning that, in our opinion, it was unpacked and inflated for the occasion. It still had little pieces of cellophane stuck to it here and there, traces of the material it came wrapped in."

"Anything concerning the body?"

"No. He was completely naked. On the other hand . . ."

"Tell me."

"It's just a personal impression."

"Tell me anyway."

"Before taking the body on board, the captain had some pictures taken which he gave to us. You want to see them?"

"No, just tell me your impression."

"Inside the dinghy the body's pallor was even more striking. He was definitely not a man of the sea."

"Ahh, Chief! Fazio tol' me to tell yiz 'at the minute you got here I's asposta tell 'im!"

"Then tell him."

Fazio arrived two minutes later, acting as if he had something important to say. He remained standing in front of the inspector.

"Chief, first we have to make an agreement."

"About what?"

"That you won't get mad and start yelling at me if every so often I have to look at my notes."

"As long as you leave out the Records Office stuff about the names of the father and mother . . ."

"All right."

Fazio sat down in the chair in front of the desk.

"Where should I begin?"

"With the owner."

"She's a lady with a nasty disposition —"

"I already know that. Go on."

"Her name is Livia . . ."

Montalbano, for no reason, gave a start. Fazio looked at him in astonishment.

"Chief, your girlfriend doesn't have exclusive rights to the name. Livia Acciai Giovannini, from Livorno, just turned fifty-two though she doesn't show it one bit. According to her, she worked as a model when she was young; but according to Maurilio Alvarez, she was a prostitute."

"And who's this Alvarez?"

"The ship's engineer. I'll get back to him in a second. So at age thirty-five this Livia meets Arturo Giovannini, a rich man and an engineer, on the beach at Forte dei Marmi. Giovannini falls in love with her and marries her. The marriage lasts only ten years, because the engineer dies."

"Of old age?"

"No, Chief, they were the same age. During a storm at sea, the poor guy falls out of the boat and —"

"Don't call it a boat."

"What am I supposed to call it, then?"

"A yacht."

"Anyway, he falls into the sea and they are never able to recover the body."

"Who told you this story?"

"The widow."

"Did Maurilio back it up?"

"We didn't talk about the accident. At any rate, she inherits the boat and continues sailing all over the place, which is exactly what her late husband used to do."

"What'd he live on?"

"Giovannini? An inheritance."

"What about the widow?"

"She inherited the inheritance."

"Seem legit to you?"

"Not really. That's all I've got on the lady. The captain's from Genoa and his name is Nicola Sperlì. When the husband was alive, Sperlì was second-in-command to the captain, whose name was . . ." He pulled a little piece of paper out of his pocket and looked at it. ". . . Filippo Giannitrapani, who he later replaced."

"Did Giannitrapani resign?"

"No, the lady fired him as soon as she inherited the boat."

"Why'd she do that?"

"According to Captain Sperlì, the two could never get along because Captain Giannitrapani had an even nastier disposition than the lady."

"And what's Maurilio say about this?"

"Maurilio says Sperlì and the lady were lovers before the husband died."

52

"I guess the husband's little fall into the sea was —"

"Not really, Chief. If they chucked him into the sea, it was for another reason."

"Explain."

"Apparently, after a couple of years of marriage the lady started making the rounds of the crew and —"

"What do you mean, 'making the rounds'?"

"Maurilio said she would take one sailor, enjoy him for a week, then move on to another. When she'd finished the round, she would start again. Except that eventually she settled on Captain Sperlì. The husband was aware of all this commotion but never said anything. He didn't give a damn. To the point that on certain nights he would sleep in a vacant cabin."

"Maurilio told you all this?"

"Yes, sir."

"Did the lady make it with him too?"

"Yes, sir."

"Isn't it possible Maurilio is bad-mouthing the owner because he wants exclusive rights to her?"

"I really don't know, Chief. On the other hand, I'm convinced Maurilio's got it in for her because she's always on his case, going down to the engine room and making fun of him, telling him she knows the engines better than he does, and telling him off for the slightest things."

"What about the rest of the crew?"

"Like Sperlì, Maurilio, who's Spanish, has always been on the *Vanna*, ever since Giovannini first bought it. The three current sailors were hired after Sperlì

53

dissolved the previous crew, because they were a constant reminder of the lady's earlier adventures."

"Let me get this straight. He dismissed everyone but not Maurilio?"

"That's right. Because Maurilio is protected."

"By whom?"

"By Giovannini's will, which stipulates that Maurilio can stay on the *Vanna* for as long as he feels like it."

"And how does Maurilio explain this clause?"

"He doesn't. He says he was very close to Giovannini."

"But not so close that he didn't let the lady take him to bed."

Fazio threw up his hands.

"Wait. And who are the other three?" Montalbano continued.

Fazio had to look again at his piece of paper.

"Ahmed Shaikiri, a North African, twenty-eight years old; Stefano Ricca, from Viareggio, thirty-two years old; and Mario Digiulio, from Palermo . . ."

Digiulio! That was the same name Vanna had claimed was her own! Was it a coincidence? Better check.

"Stop!" said the inspector. "It's too late now, but tomorrow morning I want you to get this Digiulio and bring him here."

Fazio gave him a confused look.

"Why, wha'd he do?"

"Nothing. I just want to get to know him better. Find whatever excuse you can think of, but I want him here at the station at nine o'clock tomorrow."

★ ★ ★

54

He was about to get up and go home to Marinella when the telephone rang.

"Chief, 'at'd be a lady e'en tho' she got a man's name, says she's called Giovannino an' she wantsa talk t' yiz poissonally in poisson."

"Let her in."

It was Livia Giovannini, the owner of the yacht. She came in with a big smile on her face. She was in an evening dress and looked quite elegant.

"Inspector, forgive me for disturbing you."

"Not at all, signora. Please sit down."

"I was a little disoriented the other morning when we met, and there was something I forgot to ask you. May I do so now?"

She was being more polite than the Chinese. It was obviously an act.

"Of course."

"How did you know I had a niece?"

She must have racked her brains trying to figure it out. She must have asked Sperlì for his advice and decided in the end to ask the inspector directly. Which meant that the whole business of the pseudo-niece was important. But why?

"The other morning, as I left for work, it was raining cats and dogs and the seaside road into Vigàta collapsed," Montalbano began.

And he told her the whole story.

"Did she say anything about me?"

"All she told me was your husband's name, but not his last name. Oh, and, come to think of it, she also

55

added that you're very rich and like to travel the seas. And that's about it."

The lady seemed reassured.

"Well, that's a relief!"

"Why?"

"Because sometimes the poor thing isn't really all there, and so she talks and talks and makes up the most incredible stories . . . So I was a little worried she might have . . ."

"I understand. Don't worry, she didn't tell me anything out of the ordinary."

"Thank you," said the lady, standing up and flashing a radiant smile.

"You're welcome," said Montalbano, also standing up and smiling broadly.

CHAPTER
FIVE

As he was opening the door to his house he heard the phone ringing, but when he went to pick it up it was too late. The person at the other end had hung up. He glanced at his watch: eight thirty-five.

He let off some steam by cursing the owner of the yacht a few times for having wasted his time.

He'd given Laura his home phone number and they had agreed that she would call at eight-thirty. Which was why she hadn't bothered to give him hers. So what would he do now? Call the Harbour Office? Or wait a little while, hoping she would try to call again? He decided to wait.

He changed his clothes and then went into the kitchen and opened the oven. Adelina, his housekeeper, had made a casserole of pasta 'ncasciata that could have fed four. And in the fridge, in case he was still hungry, which was unlikely, there was ready a platter of nervetti with vinegar.

The telephone rang again. It was Laura.

"I called a few minutes ago but —"

"Sorry, I was held up at the office and —"

"Where shall we meet?"

"Listen, there's a bar in Marinella —"

"No, I don't feel like it."

"Like what?"

"Like meeting you there. I don't like bars."

"Then I suppose we could —"

"Why don't you tell me how to get to your house?" she cut him off.

In fact it was the easiest thing to do, and she seemed to be a practical girl. He explained to her how to get there.

"Then let's do this. I'll come to your place, and while we're having an aperitif we can decide where to go out to dinner."

"Yes, sir."

Laura arrived half an hour later. She'd changed out of her uniform and was wearing a knee-length skirt, a white blouse, and a sort of heavy waistcoat. She had let her hair down, and it fell onto her shoulders. She was beautiful, vivacious, and very likeable.

"It's so nice here!"

Montalbano opened the French windows onto the veranda, and she went outside, enchanted.

"What'll you have?" he asked her.

"A little white wine, if you've got any."

The inspector always kept a bottle in the fridge. He took it and replaced it with another.

"Can we sit out here?"

"Absolutely."

They drank their wine sitting beside each other on the bench. But it was chilly, and when they had finished their glasses they went back inside.

"Where are you going to take me?"

"There are two possibilities. We could go to a restaurant outside Montereale, which means we'd need to take the car, or we could stay here."

She looked hesitant, and Montalbano misread her.

"You don't know me very well," he said, "but I can assure you I —"

Laura burst into laughter that sounded like pearls falling to the ground.

"Oh, I certainly wasn't thinking you wanted to . . ."

He felt a twinge of melancholy. Did she think him so old that he no longer had any desire? Luckily, however, she continued:

". . . but I must confess I'm really hungry, because I skipped lunch today."

"Come with me."

He led her into the kitchen, opened the oven, and took out the casserole. She smelled it and sighed, closing her eyes for a second.

"What do you say?" asked Montalbano. "Don't you think it's a good idea?"

"Let's stay here."

They got to know each other a little better. She told him she'd chosen a military career because her father was an admiral, now on the verge of retirement. She'd studied at the Accademia di Livorno, had sailed on the *Vespucci*, and had a fiancé named Gianni who was also a naval officer and was serving on a cruiser. She was thirty-three years old, had been in Vigàta for barely three months, and hadn't had time yet to make any friends. This was the first time since moving to Vigàta that she was eating with a man.

Montalbano, for his part, talked at length about Livia. Laura even managed to eat the *nervetti*. She had a discerning palate.

"Would you like some coffee, or a whisky?" he asked when they had finished.

"Actually, do you have any more of this wine?"

"Have you managed to identify the dead body?" Laura asked at one point.

"No, not yet. I think it's going to take a while, and it won't be easy."

"I heard he died from getting his face smashed in."

"No, they did that to him afterwards. He was poisoned."

"So . . ." she began. Then she stopped. "No, never mind," she continued. "I had this idea, but it's too silly to mention it to you . . . I've heard about you, you know. They say you're not only good, but exceptional in your field."

Montalbano blushed. And she dropped another string of pearls.

"That's fantastic! A man still capable of blushing!"

"Come on, stop it. Tell me your idea."

"I thought it might have been something like a robbery gone wrong. The man could have been mugged while strolling along the jetty. And when he tried to defend himself, the attacker picked up a stone and beat him to death. So he put him in a dinghy . . . There are so many anchored around there . . . Have you checked to see who the dinghy belongs to?"

By some miracle Montalbano managed not to blush again. He hadn't thought of this. When, in fact, it should have been his first concern. His brain was misfiring, no question.

"No, because Forensics believes the dinghy had never been used before they put the body in it."

Laura screwed up her face.

"Well, I would do a little check just the same."

Better change the subject or risk looking bad.

"Maybe you can answer a question for me. As far as you know, are there a lot of rich people who stay out at sea all year long, going from port to port and doing nothing else?"

"Are you referring to Livia Giovannini?"

"Do you know her?"

"The *Vanna* came into port here three days after I started working in Vigàta. There was a bureaucratic matter that had to be settled, and so I went on board. That's how we met. They were coming from Tangiers, but they had left some months before that from Alexanderbaai."

Montalbano balked.

"Where's that?"

"It's a small port in South Africa."

"And where were they coming from this time?"

"From Rethymno."

"And where's that?"

"In Crete. They were supposed to be going to Oran, but bad weather forced them to change course."

The inspector seemed astonished.

"Are you surprised?"

"Well, yes. It's not that the *Vanna* is a small boat, but still . . ."

"Actually, it's one of the finest yachts in the world, you know. On top of that, Livia's husband had the trim and the motors altered."

"Sperli said they have an auxiliary motor that doesn't work very well."

"Come on! I think they only use the sails for decoration. That boat is an eighty-five-foot sea serpent that originally had twenty-four berths. The cabins were later expanded and modified, so that now there are barely half a dozen beds, but in exchange they gained a great deal of space and another lounge."

"That big motorboat looks pretty serious too."

"You mean the *Ace of Hearts?* That's a Baglietto, a good sixty feet or more with two powerful GM engines and nine berths. It can go wherever it wants."

"I see you know about these things."

"It's just a personal interest, for fun."

"Listen, to get back to what we were saying, I asked you if there are a lot of rich people who —"

"Spend their lives at sea? I don't think so."

"So how else do you explain it?"

"I have no explanation for it. It may just be some mania of hers. Her husband had the same mania, and I guess she caught it from him."

Montalbano remained pensive for a moment. Then he asked:

"How could one find out how many ports the *Vanna* has called at in the past year?"

"It's probably all recorded in the captain's log."

"And how does one go about having a look at it?"

"Only the public prosecutor can do that. But he would have to come up with a brilliant excuse. Can you tell me why you're so interested in the *Vanna?* After all, it only came across that dinghy by chance."

"I can't really say why . . . I'm just curious . . . I don't know . . . There's something about it that doesn't add up."

He could hardly tell her that his suspicions had been aroused by a young woman he had met, who said her name was Vanna, the same as the yacht.

Laura didn't leave until after midnight, with the promise that they would talk on the phone the following day.

The inspector stayed up to think about the dead man.

If, as Dr Pasquano maintained, they'd rendered him unrecognizable on purpose, this meant he was someone who might be recognized. At first glance, this line of reasoning might seem worthy of Catarella or Monsieur de Lapalisse.

But it was a start.

Some poor bastard killed in this fashion did not normally, nowadays, grab the headlines, as they say in the business. The national press might give him five lines, max, and the local papers half a column. The national TV stations wouldn't even mention it, though the local ones would.

So whoever would have been in a position to identify the corpse, had they left his face intact, had to be somewhere in the vicinity of Vigàta. And the eventual identification would, therefore, have led directly to the killer. Why?

For one simple reason: because the man had been poisoned. To poison someone, you have to put the poison in something to eat or drink, there was no getting around it.

The victim must therefore have known his killer.

Maybe he was invited for an aperitif, or for dinner, as the inspector had just done with Laura, and then, when the poor guy was looking the other way . . .

Laura! She was so beautiful! But what the hell was coming over him? What was he thinking? It was hardly imaginable, at his age . . . Still, what eyes she had! And the way she looked at him!

As he was unable to think straight any more, he decided that the only thing to do was to go to bed.

"Fazio here?" was the first thing he asked, walking into the station the following morning.

"Yessir, Chief. An' there's summon ellis 'e's got together wit' 'im."

"Tell Fazio to come to my office alone."

He had just sat down when Fazio came in.

"What's Digiulio like?"

"What do you expect? He's from Palermo and —"

"I want to know if he got nervous or upset when you told him he had to come to the station."

"No. He was cool and calm. Actually, he said he was expecting it."

"He was expecting it?"

"That's what he said."

"Bring him in."

"Can I hang around?"

"No."

Fazio went out, seeming offended.

Mario Digiulio was about forty and had one of those faces that you forget one second after you've seen it.

He was wearing a black turtleneck sweater and a dirty pair of jeans. He was completely different from how Montalbano had imagined him. As Fazio had mentioned, he wasn't the least bit scared. Then, unexpectedly, as soon as Montalbano told him to sit down, he began to speak.

"So you received the complaint, eh?"

Montalbano made a vague gesture that could have meant nothing or everything.

"The bastards."

The man paused.

"The fuckin' bastards!"

Having taken in the high esteem in which Digiulio held those who had reported him, the inspector decided he needed to know a little more.

"Please tell me your version of the story."

"In Rethymno, me and Zizì went out drinking at a taverna, and there was two Greeks there who —"

"Who provoked you."

"Exactly. Zizi reacted immediately, and I went to back him up, and before we knew it, there was a brawl and —"

"You smashed the place up."

"Smashed it up? Come on! Zizi broke a couple of chairs and . . ."

Zizi. Where had he heard that name before? Someone had mentioned it in passing. But who? And when? He couldn't quite call it to mind.

"I'm sorry, but was Zizi a local?"

Digiulio gave him a look of astonishment.

"No, he's one of the crew."

"But his name's not listed in the —"

"Ah, sorry, we call him Zizi, but his real name's Ahmed Shaikiri. He's North African."

Montalbano had a flash.

"Was he the former owner's manservant?"

Digiulio's astonishment increased.

"The former owner's manserv . . . No way! Zizi signed on with us barely three months ago!"

Montalbano's brain was now firing on all cylinders.

"Could you run through the names of the other crew members for me?"

"But they weren't involved in the fight."

"Please tell me them just the same."

"Maurilio Alvarez is the engineer, Stefano Ricca's the . . ."

Montalbano stopped paying attention. Ricca! Now it had all come back to him. Vanna had said Ricca was a banker and associate of her uncle Arturo. But it was the yacht that was named *Vanna*, and Digiulio, Zizí, and Ricca were all crew members . . .

The girl had certainly been clever. What a subtle edifice of lies! Hats off!

Want to bet that what he had thought was an elaborate prank on Vanna's part actually had a precise purpose?

Meanwhile, however, he had to get rid of the sailor.

"Listen, do you by any chance have a sister named Vanna?"

"Me? No, I have a brother named Antonio."

"All right, then, you can go."

The sailor felt lost.

"What about the complaint?"

"Which one?"

"The one from the taverna's owner."

"We never received it."

"Then why did you call me in?"

"There was another complaint."

"There was?"

"Yes, by a certain Vanna Digiulio against her brother, Mario. But since you claim you have no sisters —"

"I don't claim I have no sisters, I really don't have any sisters!"

"Then it's clearly a case of two people with the same name. Good day, my friend."

The inspector was certain it wasn't Digiulio who had informed Vanna of the yacht's change of course. He absolutely needed to speak to the other crew members.

He called Fazio, who still seemed offended for having been excluded from the interview.

"Have a seat."

Montalbano stared at him for a moment. Should he tell him about Vanna or not? Now that the whole business seemed to have taken on a new meaning, wasn't it better to have Fazio as an ally?

"Do you remember when, the other day, it rained so hard that the road collapsed?"

"Yes, sir."

"Do you remember that pathetic creature I brought into the station, whose name was Vanna Digiulio?"

"Yes, sir."

"Well, you know what? Her name wasn't actually Vanna Digiulio, and she wasn't a pathetic creature but a sly little bitch who made a great big monkey out of me."

Fazio looked stunned.

"Really?" he said.

Montalbano told him the whole story.

"And what do you make of it?" Fazio asked him when he'd finished.

"Several things seem clear to me. One, that the moment I introduced myself to her as Inspector Montalbano, the girl — whom we'll keep calling Vanna for convenience — started sneezing and didn't stop."

Fazio balked.

"Wait a second. What's that got to do with it?"

"It's got everything to do with it. I would bet my family jewels that those sneezes were faked. She did it to buy time to decide whether she should tell me what she wanted to tell me. And then she immediately put me, indirectly, on the trail of the yacht."

"Why?"

"I could venture a guess. She did it for future reference."

"What do you mean?"

"If anything bad happened to her, she had given me sufficient information as to who to put the squeeze on."

"But Vanna never even showed her face to the people on the yacht."

"That's true. Because, in my opinion, something unexpected happened."

"And what was that?"

"The yacht brought a corpse on board. Which meant the presence of the police, the Harbour Office, the coroner, the Forensics department . . . Too many people, in short. And so she decided to disappear. Make sense to you?"

"Sure. But the fact remains that we still don't know what she had come to do."

"And that's why it's important to find out who she was in contact with. Someone at the Harbour Office? I don't think so. Mario Digiulio of the *Vanna?* No, definitely not. This is where I need your skills, Fazio."

"Meaning?"

"We need to talk to the other crew members, but we can't use the same set-up we did with Digiulio. You need to find a way to approach the North African, what's his name . . ."

"Shaikiri."

"Right, but his friends call him Zizì. Try to see what you can find out from him. See if you can get him drunk . . . Do they ever come ashore?"

"Are you kidding? They've been hanging out all over town."

"Well, find a way to get friendly with him." At that moment Mimì Augello appeared. Sharply dressed and smiling. "And where have you been?"

"What? You mean Catarella didn't tell you? Yesterday I took Beba and the kid to her parents' place. Can't you see the look on my face? I slept like a god last night! Finally!"

Montalbano just sat there in silence, staring at him.

"What's wrong?" Augello asked.

"I've just had an idea."

"Well, that's news! Does it concern me?"

"Yes it does. Do you feel up to wooing a fifty-year-old woman who looks forty?"

Mimì didn't hesitate for a second. "I can try," he said.

CHAPTER
SIX

He went to Enzo's to eat, feeling rather satisfied at finding, he thought, a key to understanding a little about the behaviour of the girl who called herself Vanna. He was now almost convinced that she had acted the way she did as part of a precise plan she had devised in her head when she learned that he was Inspector Montalbano.

Therefore it wasn't just a silly game, but something serious. Quite serious.

At any rate, he felt — even if he didn't exactly know why — that he was acting the way she would have wanted him to.

On the other hand, he had nothing to congratulate himself about when it came to the corpse in the dinghy. Things were practically still at square one. The inability to identify the corpse was paralysing everything. Whoever had smashed the man's face in had achieved his purpose.

And if he was a foreigner, there was no point searching all the hotels and inns in Vigàta, Montelusa, and environs. That would not only take a lot of time, but the question would remain unchanged: how do you identify someone without papers who no longer has a face?

And if, just supposing, he was a local, how was it nobody had reported him missing?

In the trattoria, the inspector did find some consolation. Fish was back on Enzo's menu, and to make up for his forced abstinence of the day before, Montalbano gorged himself. He ordered a mixed fry of mullet and calamari that could have fed half the staff at the station.

As a result, a walk along the jetty to the lighthouse became an absolute necessity. This time, too, he went out of his way, passing by the *Vanna* and the *Ace of Hearts*, which still were side by side.

No sooner had he passed them than he heard laughter and shouting behind him. He turned around to look as he kept walking.

At that moment Livia Giovannini, the *Vanna*'s owner, and Captain Sperli were descending the gangplank of the *Ace of Hearts* as a man of considerable size, a colossus a good six foot three inches tall with red hair and shoulders like a wardrobe, waved goodbye to them from the cruiser's deck. The *Ace of Hearts* might be a huge boat, but he probably had to walk with his head bent when he was below deck. Then the lady and her captain started up the gangplank to the *Vanna*.

When he got to the flat rock under the lighthouse, the inspector sat down, lit a cigarette, and started thinking about what he had just seen.

What were the owner and captain of the *Vanna* doing on board the *Ace of Hearts*?

Perhaps just a courtesy visit, a good-neighbourly sort of thing? Was it common practice for those kinds of people to do that? Given the time of day, it was also quite possible, even likely, that the *Vanna* people had been invited to lunch.

Or did they all know each other from before? Were they old friends? Or business associates or something similar?

There was only one way to find out: try to learn more about the *Ace of Hearts*.

This, however, would mean that the investigation, instead of becoming smaller and more focused, would expand by involving more people. Which was the worst thing that could happen to an investigation.

At any rate, the only way to get any information on the *Ace of Hearts* was to ask Laura, who he had something else to ask as soon as possible.

Laura! She was so . . .

Once again he got lost in his thoughts about her. He didn't like the fact that the moment she came to mind he couldn't concentrate on anything else. In his head there was only her: the way she walked, the way she laughed . . . Deep down, he felt a little ashamed of this. It didn't seem proper for a man his age. But he couldn't do anything about it.

Once inside the car, instead of going to the station, he took the road to Montelusa. Pulling up in front of the

Forensic Medicine Institute, he got out and went inside.

"Is Dr Pasquano here?"

"He's here, for what it's worth."

Which, translated, meant: He's here, but it is not advisable to go and bother him.

"Listen, all I need is a copy of the report the doctor wrote after performing the post-mortem on the disfigured corpse."

"I can get that for you myself, but you should know you can't take it away with you."

"I only need some information from it, which I can get here, on the spot, right in front of you. Please do me this favour."

"All right, but don't tell the doctor."

Half an hour later, he pulled up in front of the broadcasting studios of the Free Channel, one of the two local television stations.

"Is Zito in?"

"He's in his office," said the secretary, who knew Montalbano well.

The inspector and Zito embraced. They were old friends and were always genuinely happy to see each other.

Montalbano gave him the information he had copied down. Height, weight, hair colour, width of shoulders, length of legs, teeth ... Zito promised to make the announcement on the eight o'clock evening news and the midnight edition, which were the two most watched. Anyone who happened to call the studio in

74

response would be told to contact the Vigàta police directly.

Back in his office, he found Fazio waiting for him, looking like a beaten dog.

"What's wrong?"

"We're fucked, Chief!"

"You think that's news? What's so unusual about that? I happen to believe I've been fucked since birth. So, a little more fucked, a little less fucked, makes no difference . . . What's this about?"

"Shaikiri."

"Tell me everything."

"Well, just by chance, as I was on my way to eat, I saw Digiulio, Ricca, and Alvarez going into Giacomino's taverna. So I waited a few minutes and went in myself, and I sat down at a table not far from theirs. When I heard them talking about Zizì, I pricked up my ears. And you know what?"

"If it's bad news, I don't want to hear it. But tell me anyway."

"Zizì was arrested last night."

Montalbano cursed.

"By whom?"

"The carabinieri."

"For what?"

"Apparently, as they were going back on board last night, Zizì saw a carabinieri squad car parked near the port. He'd been drinking a lot, and he went up to the car, unbuttoned his trousers, and pissed on it."

"Is he mad? And were there carabinieri in the car?"

"Yup."

"And what happened?"

"Well, as they were arresting him, he managed to punch one of them."

Montalbano started cursing again.

"What should we do?" Fazio asked.

"What can we do? We can't very well phone the carabinieri and tell them to let him go because I need him! Listen, try and make friends with Ricca. It's the only move we can make at this point."

He and Laura had agreed the previous evening that she would call him at the office around seven o'clock, but it was now almost eight and he still hadn't heard from her. Since this time he'd had her give him her mobile-phone number, after a bit of mental tug-of-war with himself, he called her.

"Montalbano here."

"I recognized your voice."

She'd said it without any enthusiasm at all.

"Did you forget that you —"

"No, I didn't forget."

Damn, was she ever forthcoming?

"Too busy?"

"No."

"So then why didn't you —"

"I'd decided not to call you."

"Oh."

Silence fell.

And suddenly Montalbano was gripped by a hysterical fear that they'd been cut off. It was idiotic, but he could do nothing about it. Whenever he thought he'd lost his telephone connection, he went into a terrible panic, like a child abandoned in a starship adrift in space.

"Hello! Hello!" he started yelling.

"Don't shout! I'm here!" she said.

"Can you explain to me why —"

"Not over the telephone."

"Try."

"I said no."

"Well then let's meet, if you don't mind! There's also something I have to ask you about the *Vanna*."

Another pause.

This time, however, Montalbano heard her breathing.

"Do you want to have dinner together?" she asked.

"Yes."

"But not at your house."

"All right. We can go wherever you like."

"Then let's go to that restaurant in Montereale you mentioned."

"All right. Let's do this: you come here to the station, and we can take my car to —"

"No. Just tell me how to get to this restaurant. We can meet there. But give me about an hour; I still need to change."

What had got into her? Why had her mood changed so drastically? He couldn't work it out.

About ten minutes later, the phone rang.

"Ahh, Chief, Chief! Ahh, Chief!"

Bad sign. Whenever Catarella intoned these lamentations, it meant that Mister C'mishner, as he reverently called him, was on the line.

"Does the commissioner want me?" Montalbano asked.

"Yessir, Chief! An' iss rilly urgint!"

"Tell him I'm not in my office."

The commissioner was likely to tell him to come to Montelusa, which would make him miss his date with Laura.

"*Matre santa*, Chief!" Catarella wailed.

"What's wrong with you?"

"Wha'ss wrong izzat when I gotta tell a lie to hizzoner the c'mishner, iss like I'm c'mittin' a mortal sin!"

"So just go and confess!"

Forty-five minutes later, he was about to get up and leave when Fazio came in.

"Chief, I have a very good friend who's a carabiniere, and I took the liberty of —"

"What did you do?"

"I asked him what they planned to do with Shaikiri."

"And how did you explain your interest in him?"

"I told him he was a friend of mine and that whenever he drank he lost his head, and I apologized for him."

"And what did he say?"

"They released him at five o'clock this afternoon. He was charged with assault and resisting arrest. What should I do? Look for him at Giacomino's?"

"Go there at once and forget about Ricca."

★ ★ ★

He'd already stood up when the phone rang. To answer or not to answer? That was the question. Prudence suggested that it was best not to answer, but since he had given Laura this very number, he thought it might be her saying she had changed her mind, and so he picked up the receiver.

"Hello?"

"Ah, Inspector Montalbano, what luck to find you in your office! Did you just get back?"

"This very moment."

It was that humongous pain in the arse Dr Lattes, called Lattes e mieles, chief of the commissioner's cabinet, who, among other things, was convinced that Montalbano was married with children.

"Well, my friend, the commissioner has gone and left me with the task of contacting you."

"What can I do for you, Doctor?"

"We urgently need to do a complete review of documents lost during that sort of flood that damaged your offices the other day."

"I see."

"Would you have an hour or so, or perhaps an hour and a half, to devote to this?"

"When?"

"Right now. It's something we could even do over the phone. You need only have a list of the lost documents at hand. Let's start by doing a summary check, which will later serve as . . ."

Montalbano felt lost. He would have to cancel the dinner engagement with Laura!

No, he would not submit to this revenge of the bureaucracy.

But how? How would he ever wriggle out of this?

Perhaps only a good improvised performance could save him. He would do the tragic-actor thing, and he got off to a flying start.

"No! No! Alas! Woe is me! I don't have the time!" he said in a despairing voice.

It made an immediate impression on Lattes.

"Good God, Inspector! What's wrong?"

"I just now got a call from my wife!"

"And?"

"She phoned me from the hospital, alas!"

"But what happened?"

"It's my youngest, little Gianfrancesco. He's very ill and I must immediately —"

Dr Lattes didn't hesitate for a second.

"For heaven's sake, Montalbano! Go, and hurry! I shall pray to the Blessed Virgin for your little . . . What did you say his name was?"

Montalbano couldn't remember. He blurted out the first name that came to mind.

"Gianantonio."

"But didn't you say Gianfrancesco?"

"You see? I can't even think straight! Gianantonio is the oldest, and he's fine, thank God!"

"Go! Go! Don't waste any more time! And good luck! And tomorrow I want a full report, don't forget."

★ ★ ★

Montalbano was off like a rocket to Montereale.

But after barely a mile and a half, the car stalled. There wasn't a drop of petrol left in the tank. Fortunately there was a filling station a couple of hundred yards up the road.

He got out of the car, grabbed a jerry can from the boot, ran to the garage, filled the can, paid, ran back to the car, poured in the petrol, started the car, stopped at the station again, filled up the tank, and drove off — cursing the saints all the while.

When he got to the restaurant, all sweaty and out of breath, Laura was already sitting at a table, nervously waiting for him.

"Five minutes more and I would have left," she said, cold as a slab of ice.

Owing perhaps to the ordeal he had gone through to get there more or less on time, her words had the immediate effect of seriously annoying him. He was unable to control himself, and out of his mouth came a declaration he would never have thought himself capable of.

"Well, then I'll just leave, myself."

And he turned his back, went out of the restaurant, got in his car, and drove home to Marinella.

He wanted nothing more than to get into the shower and stay there for as long as it took to wash away his agitation.

Twenty minutes later, as he was drying himself off, he thought again with a cooler head about what he had done, and realized he'd committed an act of colossal stupidity. Because he absolutely needed Laura's help if he was going to get anywhere in the investigation. Indeed, the only way Mimì Augello could come into contact with La Giovannini was through Laura.

That was what happened when you mixed personal matters with work.

He decided he would call her first thing in the morning and apologize.

He no longer felt hungry. Perhaps his appetite would return if he went out for a few minutes onto the veranda and breathed some sea air. He had noticed, on the way back from the restaurant, that it was less chilly than the previous evening and there wasn't a breath of wind. So he went outside with only his underpants on. He flicked on the light for the veranda from the inside, picked up his cigarettes, and opened the French windows.

And froze.

Not because it was cold outside, but because, standing before him, speechless, eyes lowered, was Laura.

Apparently she had knocked on the door when he was in the shower and he hadn't heard it, and so, knowing he must be at home, she had walked around the house to enter from the side facing the beach.

"Forgive me," she said.

And she looked up. At once her grave expression vanished and she started laughing.

At that very same moment, as if seeing his reflection in her eyes, Montalbano realized he was in his underpants.

"Ahhh!" he screamed.

And he dashed back to the bathroom as if in a silent film.

He was so upset, so confused, that the comedy continued when, as he was standing and putting on his trousers, he slipped on the wet tiles and fell on his arse to the floor.

When at last he was able to think straight again, he emerged and went out to the veranda.

Laura was sitting on the bench, smoking a cigarette.

"I guess we've just had a quarrel," she said.

"Yeah. I apologize, but, you see . . ."

"Let's stop apologizing to each other. I owe you an explanation."

"No you don't."

"Well, I'm going to explain anyway, because I think it's necessary. Have you got any more of that wine?"

"Of course."

He got up and went out, then came back with a new bottle and two glasses. Laura guzzled a whole glass before speaking.

"I had no intention of calling you today and had promised myself that if you called me, I would say I wasn't up to seeing you."

"Why?"

"Let me finish."

But Montalbano insisted.

"Look, Laura, if there was anything I said or did yesterday that may have offended you, for whatever reason —"

"But I wasn't offended at all. On the contrary."

On the contrary? What did she mean? He'd best sit tight and hear what she had to say.

"I didn't want to see you because I was afraid I'd seem ridiculous. And anyway, it wouldn't have been right."

Montalbano felt dazed.

And he feared that anything he might say would be the wrong thing. He didn't understand what was happening.

"And so I told myself that it would be a mistake for us to keep seeing each other. It's the first time in my life this sort of thing has happened to me. It's humiliating and demoralizing. I'm completely helpless and can't do anything about it. My will counts for nothing. And in fact, when you called me, I didn't know . . . Help me."

She stopped, poured herself another glass, and drank half of it. As she brought it to her lips, Montalbano saw her eyes glisten, brimming with tears.

CHAPTER
SEVEN

Help me, she'd said. But with what? And why was she crying? How could he help her if he didn't have the slightest idea what was happening to her?

Then, all at once, Montalbano understood. And, at first, he refused to believe what he thought he'd understood.

Was it possible the same thing was happening to her as was happening to him?

Was it possible the proverbial *coup de foudre* had struck them both?

He felt angry at himself for thinking of a cliché (even if it was French), but nothing more original came to mind.

And he began to feel weak in the knees, torn in opposite directions, happy and scared at once.

Why don't you help me? he thought of asking her.

But as he was asking for help without saying anything, he wished he could embrace her and hold her tight.

And to keep from doing this, he had to make such an effort that a few droplets of sweat formed on his brow.

Then he did the only thing that could be done, if he was really the man he thought he was, even though it cost him great physical pain, a sort of knife blade piercing his chest.

"Well, given the fact that we've met," he said indifferently, as if not having understood a word she'd said or grasped the suffering in those words, "let me take advantage of the fact and ask a favour of you, assuming you're able to do it for me."

"Go ahead."

She seemed disappointed and pleased at the same time.

"My second-in-command on the force is a man named Mimì Augello, who's not only an excellent policeman but a very good-looking guy who has a way with women."

"And?" asked Laura, somewhat taken aback by that preamble.

"I thought it could be very useful to have him meet the owner of the yacht."

"I see. You think that if they hit it off, your man might manage to get some information out of her?"

"Exactly."

"Do you mind telling me why you're so fixated on this yacht? You should know that the boat has undergone many Customs inspections and they've never found anything abnormal."

"That doesn't necessarily mean anything."

"What do you mean?"

"I can't really explain, not any better than that. It's just, well, a feeling, an impression . . ."

Damn! He was supposed to be a hunting dog on the scent of its prey, not telling her the whole story of Vanna!

"And these impressions of yours, are they always correct?" she asked with a hint of irony.

"So for you she's just a rich widow whose only form of amusement is to sail the seas, ending up, from time to time, in the captain's bed?"

"Why not? What's so strange about that?"

"All right then. We'll just leave it at that."

"Wait a second. Just because I have a different opinion from yours doesn't mean I don't want to help you. Tell me how I can be of use to you."

"You have to arrange things so that Augello can meet La Giovannini."

She remained silent for a spell.

"If you don't feel like it . . ." Montalbano began.

"No, I do, I do. But before we go any further, are you sure the people on the yacht won't know who he is?"

"Absolutely certain."

"So the question is how to get them to meet. It won't be easy, you know. I'll have to bring him with me on board the yacht; but first I have to find a good excuse for boarding myself."

"I was thinking you could introduce him as some sort of specialist who needed to go on board to check something."

Laura started laughing.

"Well, you can't get any clearer than that!"

"Sorry, but I don't —"

"Let me think for a minute. I'll come up with something, I'm sure of it."

And she reached out to drink more wine. Montalbano stopped her.

"Don't you think that's a bit much, on an empty stomach? Would you like to eat something?"

"Yes," she said. Then, suddenly, "No. I'm going to leave."

She stood up.

"No, come on," said Montalbano.

She sat back down. Then stood up again.

"I'm leaving."

"Please!"

She sat back down.

She was like a puppet controlled by invisible strings.

Montalbano went into the kitchen and opened the oven. Inside a casserole were four large mullets cooked in a special sauce of Adelina's own invention.

He lit the oven and turned it on high, so the fish would warm up fast.

Then he opened the fridge, stuck in another bottle of wine, and pulled out a plateful of olives, cheese, and salted sardines. From a drawer he extracted a tablecloth, napkins, and cutlery and set these all on the kitchen table, to be taken outside momentarily onto the veranda, where he would lay the table.

At this point, wanting to make sure the mullet weren't burning, he opened the oven and grabbed the pan, and as he was still bent over he felt the weight of Laura's body press against his back as she silently embraced him, joining her hands over his chest.

He froze in that position, half bent over, feeling the blood begin to course ever faster in his body and fearing that his pounding heartbeat could be heard in the room, loud as a pneumatic drill.

He didn't even notice that the scalding-hot handles of the casserole were burning his fingers.

"I'm sorry," Laura said softly.

And immediately she detached her body from his, unfolding her hands very slowly, letting them slide away as in a long caress.

He heard her walk out of the kitchen.

Stunned, flummoxed, and numb, Montalbano set the casserole down on the table, turned on the tap to let the cold water run over his scorched fingers, then grabbed the tablecloth and silverware and went to lay the table outside.

But he stopped in the kitchen doorway.

He had only five or six more steps to take to reach the veranda and perhaps find happiness there.

But he felt scared. Those few yards were more daunting than a transatlantic crossing. They would take him very far from the life he had lived up to that moment and would certainly transform his existence completely. Could he handle that, at his age?

No, there was no time for questions. To hell with doubt, conscience, reason.

He closed his eyes, the way people do before jumping off a cliff, and walked.

On the veranda there was no sign of Laura.

At that moment he heard the sound, very near, of a car driving off.

Laura had left the way she had come.

And so he collapsed on the stone bench.

The lump in his throat almost prevented him from breathing.

★ ★ ★

He finally managed to doze off at around four o'clock in the morning. From the moment he'd gone to bed he'd done nothing but toss and turn, repeatedly getting up and lying back down. The Sicilian dictum said that of all things, the bed is best — if you can't sleep you still can rest. But that night he'd found neither sleep nor rest, only discomfort, heartache alternating with melancholy, and self-pity. "Let go of it, and it's lost", went another proverb. In his case, it was lost for ever. He remembered a poem by Umberto Saba. Normally poetry helped him get through his worst moments. In this case, however, it merely twisted the knife in the wound. The poet compared himself to a dog chasing a butterfly's shadow, and like the dog, he had to content himself with the shadow of a girl he was in love with. Because he knew, *disconsolate sadness / that such was the way / of wisdom*. But was it right, was it honest, to be wise in the face of love's richness?

An hour after he had managed to fall asleep, his eyes were wide open again. As he woke up, for a second he was convinced that he had dreamt the scene between Laura and himself in front of the oven, but then the pain of his burnt fingers reminded him that it was all real.

Laura had been wiser than him.

Wiser or more frightened?

But running away from reality didn't negate reality. It left it whole — indeed more solid than ever, because now they were both fully conscious of it.

How, when they met in front of others, would they manage to hide what they felt?

Should he take every measure to avoid seeing her? He could do this, but it would mean abandoning the investigation. That was too high a price. He didn't feel like paying it.

It was about nine in the morning, and Montalbano had already been in his office for half an hour or so when the telephone rang.

He was in a dark mood and didn't feel like doing anything. He was staring at the damp stains on the ceiling, trying to make out faces and animal shapes, but that morning his imagination had abandoned him, and the stains remained stains.

"Ahh, Chief! Iss a man says 'is name's Fiorentino."

How had Catarella finally got someone's name right?

"Did he say what he wanted?"

"Yessir. 'E wants a talk t'yiz poissonally in poisson."

"Put him through."

"I can't put 'im true in so how as 'e's on —"

"The premises?"

"Yessir."

"Show him in."

Five minutes went by and nobody appeared. He called Catarella. "Well? Where's this Fiorentino?"

"I showed 'im in."

"But he's not here!"

"He coun't be there, Chief, in so much as, juss like you said, I showed 'im into the waitin' room."

"Bring him to me!"

"Straitaways, Chief."

A short little man of about fifty, well dressed and wearing glasses, came in.

"Please sit down, Mr Fiorentino."

The man gave him a confused look.

"I beg your pardon, but my name is Toscano."

Catarella's mangling of people's surnames was getting more and more sophisticated.

"I'm sorry. Please sit down and tell me what I can do for you."

"I'm the owner of the Bellavista Hotel."

Montalbano knew the place. It had been recently built just outside town, on the Montereale road.

"A few days ago a guest arrived, saying he was going to stay for a day and a night. He went up to his room, then came back down to the lobby, had us call a cab for him, and then left, and we haven't seen him since."

"Was it you who registered him?"

"No, I drop by the hotel only once a day. My primary business is furniture. Late last night, as I was going to bed, I got a call from the night porter, who had just seen the appeal from the Free Channel for information about an unknown man who had been found dead. In his opinion, the description they gave fitted our missing client, so I decided to come and tell you."

"Thank you very much, Mr Toscano. So presumably all the information on this man is at the hotel desk?"

"Of course."

"Would you go there with me?"

"I'm at your service. I told the night porter to wait at the desk for that very purpose."

★　★　★

The document the guest had left with the porter and never picked up was not, however, much help at all. It was a European Union passport issued by the French Republic two years earlier, and it said that its bearer was Émile Lannec, born in Rouen on 3 September 1965. The tiny photograph showed the nondescript face of a sandy-haired man of about forty with broad shoulders. Montalbano felt as if he'd heard that name before. But when? On what occasion? He tried hard to remember, but couldn't come up with anything.

The passport's only peculiarity lay in the fact that there wasn't a single page that wasn't covered with stamps and entry and exit visas for various Middle Eastern and African nations. The man had certainly travelled a lot in two years! He whirled about more than a spinning top!

Émile Lannec. The inspector couldn't get the name out of his head. Then, all at once, he associated it with the sea. Lannec had something to do with the sea.

Want to bet he'd met him the time Livia had wanted to go to Saint-Tropez and he kept wanting to shoot himself in the head for living inside a cliché?

"I'm going to take this with me," he said, putting the passport in his pocket.

Gaetano Scimè, the sharp, fortyish night porter, was, on the other hand, a tremendous help.

"Was it you who signed the guest in?"

"Yes, sir."

"What shift do you work?"

"From ten at night to seven in the morning."

"And at what time did this gentleman arrive?"

"It must have been around nine-thirty in the morning."

"Why were you still on the job?"

Scimè threw his hands up.

"By chance. That day my colleague, who's also a friend, had to take his wife to the hospital and asked me to fill in for him until noon. Every so often we do these kinds of favours for each other."

"What did this man look like?"

"Just like they said on TV. I got a good long look at him when he came down to —"

"Let's proceed in an orderly fashion, please. When you saw him for the first time, how did he seem?"

The porter gave him a bewildered look.

"What do you mean?"

"Was he nervous, worried . . .?"

"He seemed perfectly normal to me."

"How did he get here?"

"By cab, I think."

"What do you mean by 'I think'?"

"I mean that from here you can't see the drop-off area and so I wasn't able to see the taxi. But when the man came in, he still had his wallet in his hands, as if he had just paid his fare, and right after that, I heard a car leaving."

"Where do you think he was coming from?"

The porter didn't hesitate.

"From Punta Raisi, the airport."

And he anticipated the inspector's next question.

"The morning flight from Rome lands in Palermo at seven. And as a matter of fact three customers from Rome arrived about half an hour after he did.

Apparently the Frenchman left the airport a little before the others."

"What makes you say that?"

"Well, he was carrying only a sort of overnight bag, whereas the others had suitcases and had to wait for them at the carousel."

"Go on."

"Anyway, he stayed in his room for about an hour, then came back down."

"Did he make any phone calls?"

"Not through our switchboard, no."

"But can one call from the rooms without passing through the switchboard?"

"Of course. But in that case, a charge for the call would show up on the guest's account, whereas there was no charge for that room."

"Do you know if he had a mobile phone?"

"I couldn't say."

"Go on."

"So the man came down and asked me to call him a cab. Since we're a bit out of the way, the taxi took about twenty minutes to get here."

"And what did he do during that time?"

"He sat down and started thumbing through a magazine. He was . . ."

The porter paused.

"No, never mind," he said. "Excuse me."

"No, you're not excused. Finish your sentence."

"When he came downstairs, he seemed to be in a different mood."

"In what way?"

"Oh, I dunno . . . More cheerful. He was humming."

"As if he'd received some good news?"

"Something like that."

"You should be a policeman."

"Thanks."

"Did he speak Italian?"

"He managed. Then the cab arrived and he left."

"And since then you haven't heard from him at any time."

"No, he hasn't called."

"Had he reserved his room in advance?"

"No."

"How do you think he knew about this hotel?"

"We advertise a lot," the manager interjected. "Even abroad."

"And have there been any phone calls for this man during this time?"

"None."

"Do you think he's ever been a guest at this hotel before?"

"I'd never seen him before."

"Do you know the cab driver who came to pick him up?"

"Of course! Pippino Madonia, co-op number 14."

"Where's his overnight bag?"

"Still in his room," said the manager.

"Let me have the key."

"Would you like me to come with you?" the manager asked.

"No, thanks."

Émile Lannec and the sea.

The room, which was on the third floor, was in perfect order. The bathroom, too. It had a small balcony from which you could see the sea and, to the left, half of the port. It was so clean, in fact, that it seemed as if no one had ever stayed in it. The little suitcase, which was slightly bigger than an overnight bag, sat unopened on the luggage stand. Montalbano opened it.

Inside were a shirt, a pair of underpants, and a pair of clean socks. In another compartment were the dirty clothes the man had taken off.

What Montalbano hadn't expected to find in it was a large pair of binoculars. He picked them up, looked at them carefully, then went out onto the balcony, pointed the binoculars at a rowing boat that was barely larger than a dot, then zoomed in.

They had extraordinary powers of magnification. The little dot immediately turned into the face of one of the fishermen on the little boat.

The inspector then pointed the lenses towards the port.

At first he didn't understand what he was seeing. Then he realized he was looking at the deck of the *Vanna* — more specifically, the door that led below decks, to the mess room.

He went back inside and emptied the suitcase onto the bed. There wasn't a single piece of paper, a document, a ticket — nothing whatsoever. He put the binoculars back inside, closed the suitcase, picked it up, went down to the lobby, and turned it over to the manager.

"Keep this."

CHAPTER
EIGHT

At the cab co-op, the moment the inspector told them who he was, they sent him to the office of the secretary, Mr Incardona, a man with the face of an undertaker, a goatee, and a tedious air about him.

"I urgently need to talk to one of your associates: Madonia, cab number 14."

"Pippino is an honest man," Incardona said defensively.

"I don't doubt that for an instant, but I —"

"Can't you just talk to me?"

"No."

"I'm sure he's working at this hour, and I don't think it's such a good idea to disturb him right now."

"I, on the other hand, think it's an excellent idea," said Montalbano, who was starting to feel his balls go into a spin. "Shall we settle this here or would you prefer to talk about it at the police station?"

"What is it you want?"

"Are you in direct communication with him?"

"Of course!"

"Then check in with him and let me know where he is at this moment."

He said it in such a tone that the other man got up without a word and left the room. He returned a few minutes later.

"At this moment he's at the taxi stand in front of the Bar Vigàta."

"Tell him to wait for me there."

"And what if he gets a fare in the meantime?"

"Tell him to make himself unavailable. I'll pay for whatever fare he loses."

There were four cabs waiting at the rank. The moment Montalbano arrived, the four cabbies, who'd been standing around chatting, turned and eyed him curiously. Apparently number 14 had spoken to his colleagues.

"Which one of you is Madonia?" the inspector asked, leaning out of his car window.

"I am," said a portly man of about fifty without a hair on his head.

Cool as a cucumber, Montalbano parked his car in one of the empty spaces reserved for taxis.

"You can't park there," said one of the cabbies.

"You don't say!" the inspector said, feigning surprise.

He opened the door to cab number 14 and sat down in front, on the passenger's side. The car's owner, looking flustered, got in on the driver's side.

"Start her up and let's go," said Montalbano.

"Where to?"

"I'll tell you once we get going."

As soon as they drove away from the rank, Montalbano started talking.

"Do you remember getting a call from the Bellavista Hotel a few mornings ago to pick up a fare?"

"Inspector, there's not a morning goes by when they don't call me to go there!"

"This particular guest was about forty, athletic, a good-looking man who —"

He remembered the passport he had in his pocket. Pulling it out, he put it under the cabbie's nose.

"The Frenchman!" he exclaimed upon seeing the photo.

"So you remember him?"

"Of course!"

"Why do you say that?"

"Because he didn't know where he wanted to go. Or, at least, that's how it seemed to me."

"Explain."

"First he asked me to take him to the cemetery. He got out, went in, stayed there about ten minutes, and then came back to the car. Then he asked me to take him to the north entrance to the port, got out, disappeared for about ten minutes, and came back. After that, I had to drive him to the train station, where he got out, was gone for about ten minutes, then got back in the car. Finally, he told me to take him to the Pesce d'Oro restaurant, where he paid me and left."

"Did you notice whether he went into the restaurant?"

"No, when I left he was just standing there, looking around."

"What time was it?"

"A little after twelve-thirty."

"All right. I want you to retrace the exact route you took that morning, then drop me off at the Pesce d'Oro. Actually, no. Let's go back to the taxi rank. I'll take my car and follow you."

He paid his fare, went and parked his own car, then returned to the spot where the cabbie had dropped Lannec off. Montalbano was convinced that all the twists and turns the Frenchman had made the driver go through had a specific purpose, that of making it impossible for anyone to know where he was actually going. A waiter stood in the doorway to the restaurant, inviting him to come in. And the inspector yielded to the temptation.

He went inside. The place was completely empty. Maybe it was too early. He sat down at the first table he came to and opened the menu.

The dishes looked promising. But writing is one thing, and cooking another.

The waiter approached the table.

"Have you decided?" he asked.

"Yes. But first I must ask you for some information."

He pulled the passport out of his pocket and handed it to the man. The waiter took a long look at the photo. Then he asked:

"What would you like to know?"

"If this man came and ate here a few days ago."

"No, he didn't come inside. But I did see him."

"Tell me everything."

"Why, may I ask?"

The man's tone had changed and the smile had disappeared from his face.

"The name's Montalbano. I'm an inspector with the —"

"Good God, yes! So you are! Now I recognize you!"

"So, please tell me . . ."

"I was standing outside the door, like I was doing just now, when a cab pulled up and this man got out. The cab drove off and the passenger just stood there in front of the curb without moving. He looked like he didn't know where to go. So I went up to him and asked him if he needed any help. And you know what he said?"

"No."

"That's exactly right. He said no. A minute later, he started walking, turned right, and after that I didn't see him any more. And that's the story. Now, what can I get you?"

Damn the moment he'd decided to eat at that stinking restaurant! Stinking and expensive to boot! The chef must have been a terminal drug addict or a criminal sadist bent on exterminating humanity. The food was overcooked, burnt, flavourless, or oversalted. He didn't get a single thing right, not even by accident.

An unlucky couple who had entered after him started showing signs of distress right after the first course. The woman raced to the toilet, perhaps to rinse out her mouth, while the man knocked back a whole bottle of wine to wash away the bad taste in his.

Back outside, he started walking, turned right as Lannec had done, then continued straight. A short while later, after crossing a side street, the north entrance of the port came into view.

He headed in that direction. The moment he was past the gate, there, right in front of him, were the *Ace of Hearts* and the *Vanna*.

Lannec and the sea.

The inspector became convinced that the Frenchman had come to the port to meet someone, not knowing he would meet his death instead. He had made a journey to go to the last appointment of his life.

Then, all at once, the bad lunch bubbled up in Montalbano's throat in a burst of burning, acidic reflux. There was only one thing to do. He walked over to a stack of wooden crates, took cover behind them, stuck two fingers into his throat, and vomited. He walked out of the port, retracing the steps he had taken, got in his car, and headed to Enzo's trattoria. He went into the toilet, rinsed out his mouth, then sat down at a table.

"What would you like?" Enzo asked.

"The best."

"Ahh, Chief! Ahh, Chief, Chief! Dacter Latte rang four times lookin' f' yiz!"

That colossal pain in the arse of the ruined documents.

"I'm not back yet. Is Augello here?"

"Nah, 'e ain't onna premmisses."

"How about Fazio?"

"Yessir, 'e's 'ere."

"Send him to me."

The first thing the inspector noticed about Fazio was that he had a black eye.

"What happened to you?"

"A fist."

"Whose?"

"Our friend Zizi's, late last night." "Sit down and tell me what happened."

"Chief, some time after nine o'clock last night I staked out a spot near Giacomino's taverna and waited for the crew of the *Vanna* to arrive. They didn't show up until past eleven."

"Who were they?"

"The whole crew. Alvarez, Ricca, Digiulio, and Zizi. I went in about half an hour later. They were talking and laughing, eating and drinking. Zizi was drinking more than the others. At one point he got up and started walking over to my table. Digiulio tried to stop him, but the Arab shoved him out of the way. I was just looking at him. So he planted himself in front of me with his legs spread and said: 'What the fuck you lookin' for, fucking cop?' He spoke pretty good Italian. He's one of those types who're always looking for trouble."

"And what did you do?"

"What could I do, Chief? I couldn't just pretend nothing was happening. Everyone in the taverna had heard him. It wasn't the kind of thing I could just let slide. I barely had time to stand up when he punched me so hard in the face I flew back against the wall. Then it was Ricca who tried to stop him, but he got punched himself. That Zizi's a bull. But I was able to take advantage of the momentary distraction when he was busy with his friend, and I dealt him a swift kick in the balls. He fell to the floor, writhing in pain, and I slapped the handcuffs on him."

"And what did you do with him?"

"I brought him here to the station and locked him up."

"And where's he now?"

"Still in the cell."

"What's he doing?"

"Sleeping."

"Let him be for now. When he wakes up, bring him to me. By the way, I want to show you something."

He pulled out the passport and handed it to Fazio, who started thumbing through it.

"And who's this Lannec?"

"I'm ninety-nine per cent sure he's the body in the dinghy."

And he told him the whole story, starting with his visit to Pasquano, continuing with his visit to Zito, and ending with his culinary nightmare at the Pesce d'Oro.

Fazio came out with one of his rare witty remarks.

"Chief, maybe the poor man did go to eat at the Pesce d'Oro but they deny it because they poisoned him themselves."

"Listen, can you recall whether we've had any dealings with this Lannec in the past?"

"I don't think so. Why do you ask?"

"Because the name doesn't seem entirely unfamiliar to me."

"You could have met him anywhere, Chief, but I'm sure it wasn't here."

"Ahh, Chief, Chief! Jesus Christ, Chief! Jesus Christ and Mary and Joseph, Chief! I can't hardly breathe, Chief!"

Catarella had knocked in his usual way, practically breaking down the door, and now he was acting like he'd been bitten by a tarantula.

"Calm down! What's going on?"

"Iss Liutinnint Sferlazza!"

"On the phone?"

"Nah, Chief, 'e's 'ere, poissonally in poisson!"

"What's he want?"

"To talk t'yiz. But be careful, Chief, eyes open at all times!"

"Why?"

"'Cause 'e ain't wearin' a uniform, 'e's in civvies!"

"And what does that mean, in your opinion?"

"'When a carabiniere's outta uniform, 'e'll make ya pay twice the norm!' A'ss wha' they say, Chief!"

"Don't worry, show him in."

Montalbano and the lieutenant had known each other for some time. And, though they might not admit it, they rather liked each other. After they shook hands, Montalbano had him sit down.

"Sorry to bother you," the lieutenant began.

"Not at all! What can I do for you?"

"I was told that a certain Mr Shaikiri, who's one of the crew of a yacht called the *Vanna*, attacked one of your men, who then arrested him. Is that right?"

106

"Yes. On the other hand, I believe the carabinieri also arrested him, when he pissed on one of your cars." The inspector paused a moment. "Then you released him almost at once."

The lieutenant seemed a little uneasy.

"That's just it. When he was inside, we received a phone call from the Regional Command, specifically about Shaikiri."

"What did they want?"

"They wanted to know if we'd arrested him."

Montalbano balked.

"How did they find out about it in Palermo?"

"Dunno."

"It really doesn't seem to me like the kind of thing that would interest the Regional Command."

"Exactly."

"Go on."

"Well, I confirmed the arrest and they told me to hold him at headquarters, saying someone would be coming from Palermo the following morning to interrogate him."

"For pissing on a squad car?"

"I was a little surprised myself. But I did as they said."

"And did this person come?"

"Actually, no. They called me back and said the person who was supposed to question him had a problem and couldn't come. And they said I should act in accordance with the law as far as Shaikiri was concerned. So I filed a report on him and then let him go."

"And why did you come to see us today?"

"Because that person finally came. He's at our station now and wants to talk to Shaikiri."

"Let me get this straight. You're asking me to turn the Arab over to you?"

"That's right."

"Out of the question."

The lieutenant grew even more uneasy.

"The person who came —"

"What's his name?"

"I don't know. Apparently he's from the anti-terrorism unit. Anyway, as I was saying, that person, as soon as he found out you'd arrested Shaikiri, had also expected . . . well, that you would refuse to turn him over to us."

"It was pretty easy to work that out. So what's he plan to do?"

"If you refuse, he's going to call the commissioner."

"And you think the commissioner will —"

"I don't think he'll be able to say no to this person."

At this point Montalbano had an idea.

"We could make an agreement."

"Let's hear it."

"I'll lend him to you for tonight. And you'll bring him back to me in the morning."

"All right," said Lieutenant Sferlazza.

Montalbano picked up the receiver and told Fazio to come to his office.

When Fazio entered, he greeted the lieutenant but showed no surprise at seeing him there.

108

Surely Catarella, seeing an enemy enter the camp of Agramante, had told everyone about it.

"Turn Shaikiri over to the lieutenant at once," the inspector said.

Fazio turned pale.

"Yessir!" he said, military style. Five minutes later, however, he came back to the inspector, looking rather agitated. "Could you tell me why you —"

"No," Montalbano snapped. Fazio turned around and left.

"Catarella, is Augello back?" he said into the phone.

"He in't onna premisses yet."

"But did he come to the office this morning?"

"Yessir, Chief."

"When?"

"When you was in conf'rince wit' Mr Fiorentino."

"Then what?"

"I put a call fer 'im true to 'im, and then, a li'l while later, 'e, meanin' Isspector Augello, I mean, 'e went out."

"Do you remember who it was that called?"

"I fergit the name, but it was a girl liutinnint from the Harbour's Office."

The inspector dropped the receiver.

Laura! She'd gotten in touch with Mimì Augello without telling him anything!

She'd stepped right over him as if he didn't exist. As if he'd never existed! He felt enraged, embittered, displeased, pained. Why had she behaved so badly? Did she want nothing more to do with him? All at once the door seemed to explode, crashing against the wall and breaking off half the plaster.

"'Scuse me, Chief, iss so urgint my 'and slipped."

"What do you want?" asked Montalbano, recovering his breath after the scare.

"Y'oughter know yer tiliphone's off the hook an' Isspector Augello called but I coun't put 'im true seein' as how as yer tiliphone in't hung up an' when I call I git a busy single 'cause iss off the hook an' —"

"Did he say he'd call back?"

"Yessir, in five minutes."

Montalbano put the receiver back in place.

The phone rang.

"Salvo?"

The inspector didn't answer right away. He had to finish counting to a thousand to dispel the irritation he felt and not lay into Augello and start yelling at him.

"Salvo?"

"What is it, Mimì?"

"This morning I got a call, supposedly on your behalf, from —"

"I know all about it."

It wasn't true. He didn't know a damn thing. But he didn't want Mimì to realize Laura had kept him out of it.

"Well, that girl, aside from being what she is —"

"What's that supposed to mean?"

"Jesus, Salvo, haven't you noticed what a wonder of nature she is?"

"You think so?"

110

A tone of indifference. With a touch of snobbery.

"Salvo, don't tell me you don't —"

"Oh, she's very pretty, no doubt about that. But to say she's a 'wonder of nature' is a bit of a stretch. At any rate, get to the point."

"I'd certainly like to get to the point with her. In fact, I think . . ." And he giggled, the imbecile!

Montalbano couldn't let him go on or he would start insulting him.

"Tell me what she's cooked up," he said.

"She said that since the *Vanna* refuelled yesterday, I could go on board with her and make a fuel check."

"I don't understand."

"I would go as the representative of the fuel importer, saying we've found some irregularities in the fuel, some residues that could impede the proper functioning of the engines. That would be the excuse."

"And what if they only let you talk to the engineer?"

"Laura rules that out. She's sure that the moment the owner hears mention of the engines, she'll want to handle it herself."

"But what the hell do you know about boat fuel?"

"Before this morning, nothing. Then at lunch Laura explained a few things to me, and in the afternoon we went and talked to someone who really knows a lot about it. Then, tonight, Laura's coming over to my place and . . ."

Montalbano couldn't stand it any longer. He slammed the receiver down, stood up, and started circling his desk, cursing like a madman.

Laura, in Mimì's house! With nobody else present! The two of them, alone!

And he'd even told Laura that Mimì had a way with women! This must surely have been enough to whet her curiosity and make her feel tempted to find out whether . . .

No. It was better not to think about the possible consequences, or he would go insane!

Damn the moment he ever thought of having Mimì meet La Giovannini!

But why was he despairing now? He had wished this on himself! He'd sought it himself, stupid shit that he was! He'd served Laura up to Mimì on a silver platter with his own two hands!

CHAPTER
NINE

He got home after a ferocious run-in with a motorist who, passing him, had come so close to his car that he very nearly ran him off the road. And so, with his head in a fog of rage, he'd followed him, caught up with him, passed him, and then screeched to a skidding halt, blocking the road crosswise with his car.

He'd got out of the car with his hair standing on end and eyes bulging, and, yelling like a madman, he'd gone on the attack, charging at the enemy. Who, meanwhile, the moment he'd seen the inspector get out of his car, had thrown his own into reverse, then accelerated forward, shooting past Montalbano, who tried to stop the car with his bare hands, very nearly falling down.

True, he had behaved just like the typical Italian driver, but as soon as he began to feel ashamed of this, he justified himself, thinking that, if nothing else, the episode had allowed him to vent his anger and frustration.

As he was opening the front door, he heard the telephone ringing.

He went to pick it up, certain — for no reason in particular — that it was someone from the station.

"Hello?"

"Forgive me for disturbing you at home," said a priest-like voice, "but as I had no news . . ."

Who was it? He didn't recognize the voice, though it sounded both familiar and unfamiliar . . .

"I'm sorry, but what sort of news do you want?"

"Of the little boy, of course!"

"Look, I think you've got the wrong number. This isn't a nursery!"

"Am I not speaking with Inspector Montalbano?"

"Yes, you are."

"I wanted to know how your little boy, your son, was doing . . . What did you say his name was?"

Shit! It was that pain in the arse Lattes! He'd told him that big lie about his young son being ill! And what had he said his name was? The only hope was to keep to generalities.

"There's been a slight improvement, Doctor. Thanks for asking. And forgive me for not recognizing you at once, but, you know, I've been so worried these days, so upset . . ."

"I understand perfectly, Inspector. And please accept my heartfelt wishes for a speedy recovery. May the Blessed Virgin keep you in her heart . . . And keep me informed — I mean it."

"It's the least I can do, I promise."

"As for those files that need to be checked —"

He hung up. He really didn't want to hear any talk about files at a time like this.

He barely had time to take his jacket off before the phone started ringing again. It was surely Lattes, who must have thought they'd been cut off.

114

And so Montalbano decided to go into tragic mode to get him out of his hair for a while. He picked up the receiver and started speaking in an angry voice.

"What is this?! My child, my flesh and blood is fighting for his life in a hospital bed and you want to talk about files? You do have a heart, don't you?"

Total silence at the other end. Perhaps he had treated the poor Dr Lattes a bit harshly. Better try to make up.

"I'm sorry if I raised my voice, but you must understand my state of mind. My poor little boy . . ."

"What the hell are you talking about?" interrupted a woman's voice, which he recognized at once.

Livia!

He felt as if the world was crashing down on his head.

He hung up at once. He was finished. Done for.

Livia would never believe that the story of the little boy was a stupid lie he'd invented from nothing.

The phone started ringing again.

No, until he collected his thoughts, he was in no condition to talk to her. He bent down and unplugged the phone.

Then he undressed on the spot, throwing his clothes to the floor as he ran to the shower.

He urgently needed to refresh his body and his brain.

Once out of the shower, he plugged the phone back in. Now he felt more in a state to talk to Livia without getting overly agitated. He would tell her the truth simply, in a clear, firm tone. And he would convince her. He dialled her number.

"Listen, Livia, I swear I don't have a son."

"I don't doubt it for a second," said Livia.

He wasn't expecting that response and felt rather relieved. It would make everything else a lot easier.

"How can you be so sure?"

"You would never have been able to keep it hidden from me for so long. Who did you think you were talking to?"

"Dr Lattes. You see, I don't know if I've ever told you this before, but he has this obsessive notion that I'm married and have at least two children. I've never been able to convince him otherwise. So I had to give him some rope. He was trying to saddle me with some bureaucratic hassle, and so I made up this story that one of my sons was gravely ill. That's all."

"That's all?" Livia repeated frostily.

"Yes."

"And aren't you ashamed of yourself?"

"Good God, Livia, why should I feel ashamed?"

"For pretending your son was gravely ill, just to —"

"What are you saying? The son doesn't exist, you said it yourself just a minute ago!"

"That doesn't matter. For Lattes, he exists."

"Livia, you're not making any sense!"

"No, my dear. I find it utterly ignoble that you used a sick child as an excuse for not doing something you didn't want to do."

"Livia, try to be rational. The child is pure fiction."

"But it still shows what kind of mind you have!"

"What do you mean?"

"I mean you could have come up with a thousand other excuses, but you didn't! It certainly would never have occurred to me to say a thing like that, and I'm not even a mother!"

Maybe Livia wasn't entirely wrong. No, in fact she was decidedly right. One should never joke about sick little children, even imaginary ones. But he didn't want to give her the satisfaction.

"Listen, Livia, I really don't feel like hearing about what kind of mind I have, especially from you."

"Why? What have I done?"

"You didn't come to my funeral."

Livia was speechless.

"What . . .? What are you talking about? Are you insane?"

"No, I'm not insane! I had a dream that I died, and you didn't feel like coming down from Boccadasse."

"But it was a dream!"

"So what? And the little boy was imaginary!"

"No, no, no! It's not the same thing at all! You were dead, and hopefully resting in peace, whereas that poor little boy is alive and you're making him suff —"

"Listen, let's forget about it. You know what I'm going to do? Tomorrow I'm going to call Lattes and set everything straight."

"Do whatever you think best, but get rid of the story about the little boy. And if it really means so much to you, I apologize for not coming to your funeral. Next time, I won't miss it."

They laughed, at last.

"How are you?" Montalbano asked.

"I'm fine. And you?"

"I'm bogged down in an investigation that's . . . Speaking of which, do you know anyone called Émile Lannec?"

"What is this? Another one of your strange jokes?"

"Come on. Do you know him or don't you?"

"Of course I do. We met him together."

"Where?"

"In Marinella."

He had no recollection whatsoever of it.

"Really? And who is he?"

"He's . . ." She started and then stopped. Then she giggled. "He's someone who's exactly like your son."

"Come on, Livia, don't . . ."

But she'd already hung up. He called back, but the phone rang and rang with no answer.

So this was how Livia would punish him for the story of the non-existent boy. Damn! The woman never pardoned him a single weakness! Not one!

As he wasn't the least bit hungry, he didn't look to see what was in the fridge or the oven. Instead he took a bottle of whisky, a glass, and his cigarettes, and went out on the veranda and sat down.

Émile Lannec.

He went back inside, picked up the Frenchman's passport, then sat down again outside.

From what he could gather from the visas, Lannec had been three times to South Africa, twice to Namibia (which he would never have been able to find on a map), four times to Botswana (which he didn't know either), and then Morocco, Algeria, Tunisia, Libya, Egypt, Lebanon, and Syria.

Except for Israel, he'd been to every country on the Mediterranean coast of Africa and the Middle East.

What line of business was Monsieur Lannec in?

Finishing his first glass, he got up, went and got a world atlas, and looked for Namibia and Botswana. They were two countries bordering on the upper regions of South Africa.

Then, all at once, the name South Africa made him remember that the *Vanna* had also been splashing about in that area. It was Laura who'd told him. He felt a twinge in his heart.

Laura!

By now she was alone with Mimì. They had definitely finished eating, and imagine Mimì not trying to take advantage of the situation! Boat fuel, right! Camouflage, right! He was worse than Don Juan! There was a good chance he already had her in his arms and was holding her tight . . .

To erase the image from his mind, he inhaled a whole glass of whisky in a single gulp.

The only hope was to concentrate, like an Indian holy man, on the question of Lannec.

He succeeded, with some effort, in doing so.

Might there be a connection between Lannec and the *Vanna?* But by the time the *Vanna* entered the port, Lannec had already been dead for a while. Besides, the arrival of the *Vanna* had been entirely unexpected. And so? Who had the *Vanna* come to meet? How was it possible he couldn't remember having met Lannec, and in Marinella of all places?

What had Livia said?

That Lannec was exactly like the little boy Montalbano had invented.

Wait a second, Montalbà, stop right there. You're getting very warm.

Livia had implied that Lannec didn't exist and was thus an imaginary person.

A flash went off in his brain. An invented character! A character in a novel!

He shot to his feet, dashed inside, and went up to the bookcase. It had to be a book he had read together with Livia.

Almost independently of his brain, his right arm reached up, and his right hand picked out a book with a light-blue cover: *Les Pitard*, by Georges Simenon. A masterpiece. He had liked the book very, very much, so much that he'd read it twice more on his own. He opened it.

There he was, the novel's protagonist, Captain Émile Lannec of Rouen, the owner and captain of a very old steamship called the *Thunderbolt*.

He leafed through the book, which now started coming back to him. It told a marvellous story. Unfortunately, however, it had nothing to do with the case currently on his hands.

Couldn't it be just a coincidence? That a murder victim happened to have exactly the same name as a Simenon character? Not really. What would be the chances of that? One in a billion?

Or could it have been a joke on the part of the Frenchman, to take a name that no one would ever recognize?

All the same, there was something worth trying: to check the passport's authenticity. But how could it be that of all the people who stamped and pasted visas on it, no one noticed that it was counterfeit? Well, actually, it was possible.

He went and sat back down on the veranda, and poured himself another glass of whisky.

But then, was it really so important to know whether the passport was genuine or not?

Was it really so critical to the investigation to know whether the victim was named Lannec, Parbon, or Lapointe?

No, he was wrong here. It was important. Very important. Because it was possible that the inspector's colleagues in France could find out whose passport had been counterfeited, and then, through them, trace back to Lannec's real identity. And it was possible it would lead to someone well known to the French authorities, and that . . .

At this point he could no longer think. He felt a little drunk. Actually, he didn't feel drunk, he was, in fact, drunk. He stood up, head spinning slightly, went back inside, closed the French windows behind him, and lay down in bed, falling asleep immediately.

At one point, around dawn, he had a dream.

He was on the terrace of an unfamiliar house, at night, with a pair of binoculars in his hands, looking through them at an illuminated window that he knew was the window of Mimi Augello's bedroom.

He'd just brought the image into focus when a black shadow descended, completely blocking the light from the window.

What could it be? Looking harder, he realized it was a large bird, a seagull, perched on a television aerial.

As he began to lose hope, the bird flew away, and the window suddenly appeared before him. He couldn't actually see the bed, but projected on the bedroom wall were two shadows, one male, one female, and they were making love . . . Mimi and Laura!

He woke up with a start.

Curiously, though, instead of getting upset over the two shadows making love, he felt perplexed over a detail of the dream: the bird, which in landing on the aerial had prevented him from seeing past it.

What did it mean? Because, if the bird was there, it must definitely mean something.

He got up, opened the French windows, and went out on the veranda.

The dawning day came armed with the best of intentions. There wasn't a cloud in the sky, not a trace of wind. The boat of his fisherman friend was already out on the water, and for a moment a trawler returning to port covered it up, making it disappear. Then, once the trawler passed, the little boat reappeared.

At that moment, in an instant, Montalbano understood the meaning of his dream.

He saw himself standing again in Lannec's hotel room, binoculars in hand, looking in the direction of the port.

What had he seen?

The hatch on the *Vanna*'s deck, leading below. But if the *Vanna* hadn't been there, what would he have seen? He would have seen the cruiser, the *Ace of Hearts*.

The day Lannec arrived in Vigàta, the *Vanna* was not yet in the port.

Wasn't it possible that Lannec had come to meet someone from the *Ace of Hearts?* And that he had received, through the binoculars — with no need for phone calls, which are always dangerous — instructions as to the hour and place of the meeting?

As soon as it was six-thirty, Montalbano looked up the number of the Bellavista Hotel and phoned.

"Is this Mr Scimè?"

"Yes. Who is this?"

"Montalbano here."

"Good morning, Inspector. What can I do for you?"

"Sorry to disturb you, but the other day I forgot to ask you something."

"I'm at your service."

"When Mr Lannec arrived at the hotel, did he ask you anything in particular that you can recall?"

The porter didn't answer right away.

"Do you not remember, or —"

"Well, Inspector, some time has gone by and . . . Wait, yes, that's it! He asked me for a room with a view of the sea . . ."

"Were those his exact words?"

"Well, now that you mention it . . . He asked me for a room with a view of the port."

Bingo!

So, to sum up. They let Lannec know that when he gets to Vigàta, he's supposed to go to the Bellavista Hotel equipped with a powerful set of binoculars and have them give him a room with a view of the port. Knowing more or less the Frenchman's hour of arrival, they put someone on guard on the *Ace of Hearts*, also equipped with binoculars or something similar.

As soon as Lannec appears on the balcony of his hotel room, the people on the *Ace of Hearts* make contact with him.

How? With binoculars as powerful as the Frenchman's, they could have written their instructions from the boat on a small blackboard.

They give him an appointment to meet them in front of the Pesce d'Oro restaurant. Lannec takes a taxi around town a few times to cover his tracks and then arrives at the appointed place. Then he starts walking, taking the first right.

At this point in his reconstruction, the inspector became convinced that just around the corner there was a car waiting to take Lannec to the cruiser at the port.

But why go there by car and not on foot, since it's only a stone's throw away?

Probably because he had to pass the Customs Police at the north entrance to the port, and in a car he was less likely to be noticed. He could, for example, partially hide his face, pretending to be asleep or reading a newspaper . . .

So the Frenchman goes on board the *Ace of Hearts*. They talk about whatever it is they need to talk about, and they probably fail to come to an agreement. And so they decide to silence him.

Or else Lannec's fate had already been sealed before he even came to Vigàta. His journey only served to lead him to his killers. And so they invite him to lunch and poison him.

But why use rat poison?

Shooting him, of course, was out of the question. The noise might attract someone's attention — say, a fisherman or sailor who happened to be passing along the quay.

Would it have made more sense to knife him?

No, a knife would have left bloodstains everywhere, which would have been easily found in any eventual investigation.

What about strangling him? A colossus like the man the inspector had seen on the *Ace of Hearts* could have done it with one hand.

This business of the poison was rather strange. It needed further reflection.

Whatever the case, once he's dead, they strip him naked, smash his face in, and deposit him somewhere. On the morning of the storm, they decide it's the right time to get rid of the corpse.

They start up the engines, take a few spins around the port, meanwhile inflating a brand-new dinghy, put the victim's body in it, and when they reach the lighthouse at the tip of the eastern jetty, they lower the dinghy into the water, certain that the current will take it out to sea.

But there's an unlucky hitch. The *Vanna*, as it's heading towards the port, comes across the dinghy.

Montalbano felt satisfied with his reconstruction.

Most of all, he felt pleased that he'd been able to go a whole hour without thinking of Laura — Laura, who was opening her eyes and smiling at Mimì, as she lay beside him in bed . . .

CHAPTER
TEN

He got into his car and headed straight for Montelusa Central Police, without passing by the station.

Luckily for him, the office he needed to go to was on the opposite side of the building from the commissioner's. At least there was no danger of running into that colossal pain in the arse Lattes.

But sooner or later their paths were bound to cross. How was he going to resolve the problem once and for all? He'd promised Livia he would tell him the truth — that is, that he wasn't married and had no children, and was a bachelor though he'd been with the same woman for many years. But hadn't he already told him this at least five times in the past, and each time he seemed not to hear him, so that when next they met he was immediately back to square one and asking the inspector how his family was doing? Trying to convince Lattes was a waste of breath.

Perhaps, however, there was a solution: to show up in front of Lattes one fine morning, dressed in deep mourning and unshaven, and say, between sobs, that his wife and sons had died in a car crash. Yes, that seemed to be the only solution.

But wouldn't Livia make a big stink? Wouldn't she accuse him at the very least of having wiped out his whole family? Was it worth the risk?

To say nothing of the fact that there would be no mention of the crash in the papers.

No, he had to find another solution.

Meanwhile, he'd arrived at Montelusa Central. Going in through a back door, he climbed two flights of stairs and stopped in front of a small table at which a uniformed policeman he knew was seated.

"Is Inspector Geremicca in?"

"Yes, the inspector's in his office. You can go in."

Montalbano knocked and entered.

Attilio Geremicca was about fifty years old, thin as a beanpole, and smoked foul-smelling cigars. Montalbano was convinced he had the things specially made for him out of a blend of chicken shit and tobacco. Geremicca was standing and looking at a fifty-euro note through a sort of gigantic microscope on a tall counter.

Looking up, he saw Montalbano and went up to him with open arms. They embraced, genuinely happy to see each other.

After chatting a bit, Geremicca asked Montalbano if he needed anything, and the inspector, after handing him Lannec's passport, told him the whole story.

"And what do you want from me?" Geremicca asked.

"I want you to find out if that passport is authentic or not."

Geremicca studied it carefully while lighting another cigar.

Thinking he would never manage to hold his breath for the whole time, Montalbano pretended to sneeze, giving himself an excuse to put his handkerchief over his nose and keep it there.

"It's not easy to say," Geremicca commented. "But if it's not authentic, it was made, at least in part, by a real master. Look how many borders it's crossed without arousing suspicion."

"So you're inclined to say it's authentic."

"I'm not inclined to say anything. Do you have any idea how many people there are who travel for years and years with phony passports? Hundreds! And this Lannec . . ."

"Actually, as far as the name is concerned, there's something you ought to know that might be important."

"What's that?"

"I've discovered that this Émile Lannec, born in Rouen, has the same name and birthplace as the protagonist of a novel by Simenon. Could that be of any use to you?"

"I can't say yet. Listen, could I hang on to this for a few days?"

"Not for too long. One week enough?"

"Yes."

"What do you want it for?"

"I want to show it to a French colleague of mine who is quite the specialist on the subject."

"Will you post it to him?"

"No, there's no need."

"But how will your colleague know whether the paper, the stamps —"

"A passport's not a banknote, Salvo!" Geremicca said, smiling. "Normally passport counterfeiters work with authentic documents obtained illegally or stolen from an office while still blank. That's why I said a minute ago that it looked to me, but only in part, like the work of a master. Anyway, if my French friend needs any further clarification, there's always the Internet. Don't worry, a week should be more than enough."

The first thing he did on entering the station was to call Fazio into his office.

"Have the carabinieri brought Shaikiri back?"

"Yes, sir. He's here."

The inspector was about to tell him to bring him into the office when the telephone rang.

"Wait a second," he said, picking up the receiver.

"Ahh, Chief! That'd be proxetutor Gommaseo onna line wantin' a talk to . . ."

"All right, put him on."

"Montalbano?"

"What can I do for you, sir?"

"Listen, I wanted to let you know that yesterday afternoon a rather irritated Mrs Giovannini, owner of the *Vanna*, descended on me . . . Fine-looking woman . . . you know who I mean?"

"Yes I do, sir."

"She must be a dominatrix, I'm sure of it."

Montalbano didn't understand.

130

"A what? Dominate what?"

"She dominates her partner, my friend! You can bank on it. In the intimacy of her bedroom, the lady dresses up in leather trousers and spiked heels and uses whips on her lover, who she treats like an animal and probably puts a bit in his mouth and rides him like a horse . . ."

Montalbano felt like laughing but managed to restrain himself. For a brief moment, the prosecutor's words conjured in his mind an image of Mimí naked and sprawled out on the floor like a bearskin rug, with La Giovannini grinding her heel into his back . . . Ah, the sexual fantasies of Prosecutor Tommaseo! Who, to all appearances, had never been with a woman. With all these fantasies about La Giovannini in his head, his eyes were probably popping out and his hands trembling at that very moment, drool collecting at the corners of his mouth.

"Anyway, as I was saying, she came by yesterday and adamantly insisted that it's unreasonable to force her to keep her boat in the port for so long. She said we're engaging in an obvious abuse of power, they have nothing to do with that man's murder, and all they did was recover a dead body adrift on the water . . . And, indeed . . ."

"So what's your conclusion?"

"Well, I just wanted to let you know that I'm rather inclined to let them leave whenever they like."

"I wouldn't be so —"

"Look, Montalbano, we have nothing on them to keep them here any longer. And why should we? I'm

131

convinced that neither she nor any member of her crew had anything to do with the murder. If you disagree, you should tell me. But you have to give your reasons. And so?"

Since Tommaseo knew nothing about the girl who called herself Vanna and the suspicions she had aroused in Montalbano's mind concerning the yacht, his assumptions were unfailingly correct. But the inspector could hardly allow the yacht to get away.

"Could you give me two more days?"

"I'll give you one more day. That's the most I can possibly grant you. But you have to tell me why you need the time."

"Could I come to your office the day after tomorrow?"

"I'll be waiting for you."

He would have to make do with a single day. After hanging up, he told Fazio to go and get Shaikiri.

A single day. But if he was clever enough, maybe he could detain Mrs Giovannini for another week.

Ahmed Shaikiri was twenty-eight years old, and it was hard to tell that he was North African, because he looked exactly like a Sicilian sailor. He seemed sharp and had intelligent eyes and a natural elegance about him.

Montalbano immediately liked him.

"Stick around and take a seat," the inspector said to Fazio, who was getting ready to leave.

"You, too, sit down, Shaikiri."

"Thank you," the Arab said politely.

Montalbano opened his mouth to begin speaking, but the man didn't give him the time and spoke first.

"Before anything else, I really would like to beg this gentleman's pardon for having punched him. Please accept my apologies," he said in perfect Italian, turning to Fazio. "Unfortunately, whenever I drink wine —"

"Sicilian wine," Montalbano interrupted.

Shaikiri gave him a confused look.

"I don't understand."

"I mean it must be Sicilian, or maybe Greek wine that has this effect on you."

"No, look, I —"

"Listen, Shaikiri, you're not going to tell me that the wine you drink in . . . I dunno, let's say Alexanderbaai, South Africa, just to name the first city that comes to mind, gets you so easily drunk."

Shaikiri looked dumbfounded.

"But I . . ."

"Let me put it more clearly. The wine you drink in Alexanderbaai doesn't make you start punching the local police or carabinieri or whatever it is they have down there. Isn't that right?"

Montalbano's words had a double effect. First, on Fazio, who immediately pricked up his ears, realizing that the inspector wasn't just blathering at random but had a specific purpose in mind. And second, on Shaikiri, who visibly gave a start at first and then seemed to pretend he didn't understand.

"All right, you can go," Montalbano cut things short.

Shaikiri seemed more bewildered than ever.

"You're not going to charge me?"

"No."

"But I provoked and started punching a —"

"We'll let it slide this time. You've already been charged by the carabinieri, haven't you?"

"Yes."

"And you were questioned yesterday at their base, right?"

"Yes."

Montalbano felt himself trembling inside. He'd reached the point where he had to say the decisive thing that would let him know whether he was right in his surmise or mistaken all down the line.

"If you see her again, and I'm sure you will see her or at least hear from her again, please give her my best."

Shaikiri turned pale and squirmed in his chair.

"Who am I supposed to —"

"The young lady . . . I'm sorry, the person who, well, let's say 'questioned' you yesterday."

A few beads of sweat appeared on Shaikiri's forehead.

"I . . . I don't understand."

"It doesn't matter. Good day."

Then, turning to Fazio:

"Let him go."

Naturally, as soon as Shaikiri had left, Fazio raced back to Montalbano's office.

"Would you please tell me what's going on?" he asked.

"After talking to Lieutenant Sferlazza of the carabinieri, I became convinced that the person informing the so-called Vanna about what was happening on board the yacht was Shaikiri. He had to be the one who told her that they had to change course because of the storm and head to Vigàta."

"And how would he have done that?"

"I dunno. Maybe with a satellite phone. And so Vanna got moving so she could meet him, but the dinghy with the corpse sent that rendezvous up in smoke. So Shaikiri got himself arrested by the carabinieri, revealed who he was, and they immediately put him in touch with Vanna. And yesterday she was finally able to talk to him."

"And why did he punch me, too?"

"Because he's a smart young man. He wants his friends to think that the local wine always has the same effect on him. He gets in fights with all kinds of cops, whether carabinieri or not."

"So then who's this Vanna?"

"Sferlazza said something about the anti-terrorism unit, but I think he was lying. There's definitely something shady going on on board that yacht. And Vanna is on their case. And you know something else?"

"What?"

"In my opinion the people on the *Ace of Hearts* are up to their necks in the business of the corpse in the dinghy."

Fazio sat down.

"Tell me everything," he said wearily.

"How should we proceed?" Fazio asked after he'd heard the whole story.

"Well, while we know plenty about the *Vanna*, we are totally in the dark as to the *Ace of Hearts*. So we need to start informing ourselves immediately."

"I can look into that myself."

"Fine, but you have to start somewhere. Tell you what. Go to the Harbour Office and talk to Lieutenant Belladonna, who is a woman. Have her fill you in on everything they know about the *Ace of Hearts*. Go there right now, in fact. The less time we waste, the better."

He didn't feel like going there personally in person. He couldn't bear the idea of seeing Laura, especially after she'd surely spent the night with Mimì.

"And what if she asks me why I need all this information?"

"I think you can speak freely with her. Tell her we have strong suspicions the killing occurred on board the cruiser."

It was half-past twelve when the outside line rang. It was Mimì Augello.

"She's taken the bait."

"In what sense?"

"In the way that we wanted. Laura took me on board and then left immediately. I told the lie about the fuel and had them fill a jerry can with a sample. La Giovannini didn't leave me alone for a minute. Among other things, she convinced me she really knows her engines."

"Where are you calling from?"

"From the quay. I came off the boat to put the jerry can in my car. But I have to go on board again because I've been kindly invited to stay for lunch. The lady has set her sights on me and won't let up."

"What do you think you'll do next?"

"The captain will also be there at lunch, but I'm hoping to find a moment where I can ask her out to dinner, alone, tonight. I think she'll accept. I get the impression the lady wants to eat me alive."

"Bear in mind, Mimì, that La Giovannini has protested to Tommaseo that the yacht is being detained illegally. Tommaseo wanted to give her permission to leave right away, but I got him to give me one more day. So time is running out. Got that?"

"Got it."

It was a beautiful day. The sky looked as if it had received a new coat of paint during the night, and yet the moment he got in his car to go to eat at Enzo's, a sudden bout of melancholy descended on him with such force that everything — sky, buildings, people — turned grey all at once, as on the darkest of winter days.

Even his appetite, already skimpy, suddenly deserted him. No, there was no point in going to the trattoria; the only thing to do was to go home, unplug the telephone, undress, get in bed, and pull the sheets up over his head and blot out the whole world. But what if, for example, Fazio had something important to tell him?

He got out of the car and went to see Catarella.

"If anyone asks for me, I'm at home. I'll be back at work around four."

He got back in the car and drove off.

Naturally, though covered so thoroughly by the bedsheets he looked like a mummy, he couldn't fall asleep.

There was no wonder as to the cause of this bout of melancholy. He knew it perfectly well. It even had a name: Laura. Perhaps the moment had come to consider the whole matter in the most dispassionate manner possible, provided, of course, that he could manage to be dispassionate.

He had liked Laura a great deal at first sight. He'd felt something emotional, something deep, almost moving, the likes of which he hadn't felt since the days of his youth.

But this probably wasn't something that happened only to him. No doubt it happened to a great many men well past the age of fifty. But what was it? Nothing more than a desperate, and useless, attempt to feel young again, as if the feeling alone could wipe out the years.

And this was precisely what was muddying the waters, because he could no longer tell whether this feeling was real and genuine or false and artificial, since it arose in fact from the illusion of being able to turn the clock back. Hadn't the same thing happened to him with the equestrienne? With Laura, however, he hadn't had a chance to put his thoughts in order. He was letting himself be carried away by the current he himself had created when the unforeseeable had happened.

That is, when Laura had told him she felt the same attraction to him. And how had he reacted?

He'd felt simultaneously scared and happy.

Happy because a young woman loved him? Or because he'd succeeded, despite his age, in making a young woman fall in love with him?

There was a pretty big difference between the two.

And didn't fearing the consequences actually mean that the intensity of his feeling was weak enough to allow him still to consider it rationally?

In matters of love, reason either resigns or sits back and waits. If it's still present and functioning, and forces you to consider the negative aspects of the relationship, it means it's not true love.

Or maybe that wasn't quite the way things were.

Maybe the fear had arisen in him from the very feeling he'd had when he heard Laura's words. The sense, that is, that he wasn't up to the task. That he no longer had the strength to bear the violence of a genuine emotion.

This last consideration — perhaps the most accurate so far — gave rise to a suspicion in him.

When he'd thought of using Laura to put Mimì in contact with the owner of the yacht, did he not, perhaps, have another, inadmissible, intention?

Feel like saying it out loud, Montalbà?

Didn't you know that by introducing Laura to Mimì, the whole thing risked taking a different turn? Had you not factored this in? Or — and here, please try to be sincere — had you factored it in to perfection? Didn't you have a secret wish that Laura would end up in Mimi's bed? Didn't you practically pass him off to her with your own two hands?

For this last question he had no answer.

He lay in bed for another half-hour or so, then got up.

But he'd achieved a fine result. His melancholy, instead of dissipating, had increased and turned into a black mood. "Black mood at sunset", as Vittorio Alfieri once put it.

CHAPTER
ELEVEN

"Ahh, Chief, Chief! Dacter Pisquano phoned lookin' f'yiz sayin' as how as 'e's lookin' f'yiz a talk t'yiz poissonally in —"

"Did he say whether he'd call back?"

"— poisson. Nah, Chief. 'E said sumpin' ellis."

"What'd he say?"

"'E said as how y'oughter call 'im atta Isstitute a Lethal Midicine."

"It's Legal Medicine, Cat, not lethal medicine."

"Iss whatever it is, Chief, 'slong as y'unnastand."

"Call the Institute and when you've got the doctor on the line, put him through to me."

About ten minutes later, the telephone rang.

"What's going on, Doctor?" the inspector asked.

"Are you surprised?"

"Of course. A phone call from you is so rare an occurrence, we're liable to get an earthquake tomorrow!"

"Well, aren't you the wit! Listen, since the mountain didn't come to Mohammed, Mohammed has gone to the mountain."

"But in this specific case, the mountain had no reason to go to Mohammed."

"That's true. Which is why this time it was up to me to come and annoy you."

"Go right ahead. It'll make up for all the times I've done the same to you."

"Not so fast, my friend! Don't get clever with me! I've still got a lot of credit left! You can't compare the incessant, humongous aggravation I've had to put up with, with this one —"

"OK, OK. Don't keep me on tenterhooks."

"See what old age does? You used to hate clichés and now you're using them! At any rate, I'm writing the report on the unknown corpse found in the dinghy."

"While we're on the subject, I should tell you that he's no longer unknown. I found his passport, which says his name is Émile Lannec, French, born at —"

"I couldn't give a flying fuck."

"About what?"

"About his name or the fact that he's French . . . To me he's just a corpse and nothing else. I wanted to tell you that I performed a second post-mortem because there was something that had left me wondering."

"Namely?"

"I'd noticed some scars, despite the fact that they'd smashed up his face . . . It looked like he'd had it remade."

"What?"

"Is your question an expression of surprise or do you want to know what he'd had remade?"

"Doctor, I understood perfectly well that he'd had his face remade."

"What a relief! You see, there are a few things you can still grasp."

"Are you sure he'd had such an operation?"

"Absolutely certain. And it wasn't just a snip here and a tuck there, mind you, but a major transformation."

"But why then —"

"Listen, I'm not interested in your whys and wherefores. It's not up to me to give you the answers. You have to find them yourself. Or, at your advanced age, are your brain cells so deteriorated that —"

"You know what I say to you, Doctor?"

"No need to tell me. I can intuit exactly what you want to say to me, and I return the compliment with all my heart."

When he carefully considered the information Pasquano had just given him, it didn't change the general picture much.

What difference did it really make whether the Frenchman's face was the one Mother Nature had given him or a fake, remade face?

Whoever killed him wanted to make it so that the dead man's face, whatever it was at that time, couldn't be recognized. Why?

He'd already dealt with this question, but maybe it was best to come back to it for a minute.

Especially because, searching Lannec after he was dead, the killers realized he didn't have his passport on him. And so they rightly concluded he'd left it at the hotel. Therefore, if the victim's face appeared on television or in the newspapers, it would be easy for the hotel people to . . .

Wait a second, Montalbà!

He grabbed the phone book, looked up the number of the Bellavista Hotel, and dialled it.

An unknown voice picked up. It must have been the day-shift porter.

"Inspector Montalbano here."

"What can I do for you?"

"Is Mr Toscano there?"

"He called to say he wouldn't be in today. You can reach him at the furniture factory."

"Could you please give me the number?"

The man gave it to him, and the inspector dialled it.

"Mr Toscano? Montalbano here."

"Good afternoon, Inspector."

"There's something I need to ask you, something very important."

"Go right ahead."

"Pay close attention. The night that Lannec arrived, did anything strange happen at the hotel?"

Toscano paused to think for a moment, then spoke.

"Well, actually, yes, now that you mention it . . . But it was something that . . . which I don't . . ."

"Go on, tell me."

"You see, the hotel is rather isolated. One night, in high season, three months after we'd opened for business, burglars broke in and took the safe in which we keep our customers' money and valuables."

"But wasn't the night porter on duty?"

"Of course he was. But it was three in the morning, and it's always very quiet at that time of the night and so Scimè had lain down on a little bed in the room just behind the front desk . . . They must have drugged him, because he woke up two hours later with a terrible headache . . ."

How come he'd never heard a thing about this?

"Did you report the burglary?"

"Of course. To the carabinieri."

"And what was their conclusion?"

"Since there'd been no break-in, only the theft of the safe, the carabinieri concluded the burglars had an accomplice staying at the hotel as a guest, and that he must have drugged the porter with a gas canister and opened the door for his partners. But they didn't take the investigation any further than that. It was a good thing we were insured!"

"And what happened the other night?"

"Well, after the robbery we hired a night guard who makes the rounds outside the building every half-hour. On the night in question, he saw a car stopped with its lights off, outside the back door of the hotel. But the moment he approached, the car drove away in a hurry. That time, though, since nothing actually happened, we didn't bother to report it . . . Do you think it might have a connection to the murder?"

Montalbano had no intention of telling him exactly just how close a connection it had.

"Absolutely not. But it's all grist for the mill, you know."

Damn! Pasquano was right! The older he got, the more he spoke in clichés!

So, to return to the matter at hand, someone from the *Ace of Hearts* had tried to recover Lannec's passport and hadn't succeeded. As soon as they'd seen the night guard they'd sped off. It was too dangerous.

Because once they were identified as being from the cruiser, the murder investigation would certainly have led back to them. They couldn't risk it.

But they'd had the right idea: the passport was the only thing that might make it possible to identify the dead man. Getting rid of it would have meant the corpse would probably remain for ever nameless. And since they'd failed to get their hands on it, they had to content themselves with smashing in the dead man's face.

Want to bet the false face was better known than the real one?

The inspector decided it was best to inform Geremicca of the surgically remade face. He was about to phone him when Fazio came in.

"I've spoken to the lieutenant," said Fazio.

Montalbano immediately felt envious.

Fazio had had a chance to see Laura, to be close to her, to hear her breathing and talk to her . . .

"What did you find out?" His voice sounded choked.

"You stuffed up?" Fazio asked.

"No, it's nothing, my throat's just a little dry. Tell me."

"First of all, I found out that this *Ace of Hearts* turns out to belong to an Italo-French company that —"

"That sort of thing happens all the time. It's unlikely it would belong to an individual. They do it to pay less tax. And what's this company's business?"

"Import-export."

"Of what?"

"A bit of everything."

"And what do they need a monster motorboat like that for?"

"The lieutenant told me the company operates all over the Mediterranean, from Morocco and Algeria to Syria, and even Turkey and Greece . . ."

The places stamped in the Frenchman's passport.

"The lieutenant also said that it's not the first time the cruiser has called at the port of Vigàta. Normally, though, it stays only for a day, two at the most. This time, however, it's stayed longer because they're waiting for someone from outside to come and look at the engines, which have been misfiring."

"But wouldn't it have been better for them to get an aeroplane?"

"What do you want me to say, Chief? It's their business."

"The other day, I saw a sort of colossus on their deck, saying goodbye to the owner of the *Vanna* and the captain."

"He's the company's chief executive. His name's Matteo Zigami, and he's six foot three and a half."

"How many people are there on board?"

"Five. Zigami, his secretary François Petit, and a three-man crew. The company's called MIEC."

"What's that stand for?"

"Mediterranean Import-Export Corporation. According to Lieutenant Garrufo —"

"Ah, so you didn't speak to Lieutenant Belladonna?"

"No."

"She wasn't there?"

"No. The marshal at the entrance to the Harbour Office told me she'd been up all night . . ."

What? Was it possible? So even at the Harbour Office they knew that she and Mimì . . .? Jesus, how embarrassing!

". . . due to the sudden landing of about a hundred illegal immigrants, and she'd had to stay on duty till dawn."

So she hadn't spent the night at Mimì's place! She'd never even had the chance to set foot there!

Somebody set a couple of bells ringing in his head. But it wasn't just bells; there were also about a thousand violins. He could see Fazio's mouth opening and closing but couldn't hear what he was saying. Too much noise.

He shot to his feet.

"Well done, Fazio!"

Fazio, utterly flummoxed, let the inspector embrace him, wondering if his boss hadn't suddenly lost his mind. Then, when Montalbano finally let go of him, he ventured to ask in a thin little voice: "So, how should we proceed?"

"We'll deal with that later, we'll deal with that later!" As he was leaving, Fazio heard the inspector start singing. Then, still practically singing, Montalbano told Geremicca about the reconstructed face.

★ ★ ★

All at once he was in the grip of a gargantuan hunger.

He glanced at his watch. It was already eight-thirty. The violins had stopped playing, but the bells kept on ringing, though at a lower volume.

He got up, went out of the office, and walked past Catarella with his eyes closed, looking like a sleepwalker. Catarella got worried.

"You feel OK, Chief?"

"I feel great, Cat, great."

So they were worried about his health? But at that moment he felt like a kid again! Twenty years old. No, better not exaggerate, Montalbà. Let's say forty.

He got in the car and headed home to Marinella. As soon as he was inside he raced to see what was in the fridge. Nothing. Totally empty, except for a plate of olives and a little bowl of anchovies. He ran to the oven and opened it.

Nothing there either. Only then did he notice a note on the kitchen table.

Sints I don feel so good coz I got a headache I cant cook and gonna go home. My appalogies, Adelina.

No, there was no way he could get through this special night on an empty stomach. He would never be able to sleep. The only solution was to get back in the car and go to Enzo's.

"What? Adelina let you down tonight?" Enzo asked when he saw him come in.

149

"She wasn't feeling well and couldn't cook. What can you give me?"

"Whatever you like."

He started with a seafood antipasto. Since the *nunnati* were crispy as can be, he ordered a second side dish of them. He continued with a generous helping of spaghetti in squid ink. And he ended with a double portion of mullet and striped sea bream.

When he came out, he became immediately convinced of the need for a nocturnal stroll to the lighthouse. This time he didn't go out of his way to check on the cruiser and the yacht. The jetty was deserted. Two steamers were berthed there, but they were completely in the dark. He took his walk slowly, one step at a time.

He felt at peace with himself that evening. The sea was breathing gently.

He sat down on the flat rock and lit a cigarette.

And he concluded that as a cop, he was quite good, and as a man, he was half-assed.

Because as he was approaching the lighthouse, he'd done nothing but think about Laura and the way he'd reacted when he learned she hadn't gone to Mimì's place after all.

His happiness had suddenly evaporated when a thought had popped into his head — namely: and just how do you see this girl, Montalbà? You were so certain that the same person who the day before hadn't wanted to stay alone with you because she was scared by what she was beginning to feel was ready, the very next day, to fall inexorably into Mimi's arms! And you were despairing over it!

How could you be so certain? It surely wasn't because of Laura's honest, forthright behaviour with you.

And so? Wasn't this conviction of yours based solely, perhaps, on a prejudice concerning not only Laura but the very nature of all women?

Namely, that in the end it takes very little, or nothing at all, to persuade a woman to say yes? Wasn't this what you were thinking inside? And isn't this actually the dick-brained mistake of someone who simply doesn't understand women? Need proof? Just tell Laura you thought she would end up in Mimi's bed, and see how she reacts. Punches and slaps at the very least, and a demand that you apologize.

"Laura, I'm so sorry," he said aloud.

And he promised himself he would call her in the morning.

After smoking another cigarette, he stood up and started walking back. Halfway down the jetty he heard the sound of a patrol boat crossing the harbour. He turned around to look.

A Coast Guard patrol was shining a floodlight on a barge lingering on the water.

He could see a dark mass inside the barge. There were about thirty illegal immigrants clinging to one another, frozen and hungry.

He also saw that two powerful searchlights had been lit on the western quay, the one where the refugees usually disembarked. His colleagues from the police force must already be there with buses, ambulances, cars, and a crowd of rubberneckers.

He'd once happened, by bad luck, to get caught right in the middle of a landing of the poor wretches and since then had decided never to be present for another. Luckily his own police department was not part of the force assigned to the problem; Montelusa dealt with it directly.

Seeing them, he could tolerate those eyes bulging in fear over what they had been through and what uncertainties awaited them; he could tolerate the sight of gaunt bodies that couldn't stand up straight, of trembling hands and silent tears, of little children whose faces became wizened and old in an instant . . .

What he could not tolerate was the smell. But maybe there was no smell at all; maybe it was just his imagination. But, real or not, he smelled it just the same, and it made his knees buckle and pierced his heart.

It wasn't the smell of filth. No, it was something completely different. It arose directly from their skin, ancient yet present, a strong smell of despair, of resignation, of misfortunes and violence suffered with heads bowed.

Yes, what that heart-rending smell communicated was the sorrows of the injured world, as Elio Vittorini had put it in a book he'd once read.

And yet this time, too, his footsteps, disobeying his brain, headed towards the western quay.

When he arrived, the patrol boat had just berthed. He kept a distance, however, sitting down on a bollard.

It looked like a half-silent movie. By now the people in charge knew what they had to do; there was no need to give or receive orders. One heard only sounds: car doors slamming, footsteps, ambulance sirens, vehicles driving away.

And there were the usual TV cameramen, even though there was no point in re-filming a scene already too familiar. They could have easily rebroadcast the material they'd shot a month before, since it was exactly the same, and nobody would have noticed.

He waited until the floodlights suddenly went out and the darkness seemed to thicken. Then he stood up, turned his back on the three or four shadows that remained talking to each other, and headed towards his car.

All of a sudden he clearly heard some footsteps running up to him from behind.

He stopped and turned around.

It was Laura.

Without knowing how, they ended up in each other's arms. She buried her face in his chest, and Montalbano could feel her trembling all over. They were unable to speak.

Then Laura broke free of his embrace, turned her back to him, and started running until she disappeared into the darkness.

CHAPTER
TWELVE

The first thing he did when he got home was unplug the telephone. God forbid Livia should call. No way he could carry on a conversation with her. Every syllable of his would be a burning twist of the knife of remorse and shame for being forced to lie.

"What did you do today?"

"The usual things, Livia."

"All right, but tell me anyway."

And he would go from one whopper to the next, each one bigger than the last. And then the hesitations, the half-spoken words . . . No, at his age, it really wasn't right.

He had to reflect calmly, and as lucidly as possible, on the miracle that had happened to him, and then make a decision that was clear and definitive. And if he decided to submit to the miracle, to a grace that both thrilled him and filled him with dread, he owed it to Livia to tell her at once, face-to-face.

But at that moment he wasn't in any condition to think rationally. The excitement turned his thoughts into one big jumble. If, earlier, he'd heard bells and violins, now, after what had happened on the quay, the music had disappeared, and all he heard was his blood coursing swift and limpid as an alpine stream, his heart beating fast and strong. He needed to release all this energy, which continued to build up almost unbearably with each minute that passed.

He took off his clothes, put on his trunks, went down to the beach as far as the line where the sand was dense and compacted, and started running.

When he got back home, his watch said just past twelve-thirty.

He'd run for two hours straight without stopping for a minute, and his legs ached.

He slipped into the shower and stayed there a long time, then went to bed.

Exhausted from the run. And from happiness.

Which, when it is truly great, can cut your legs out from under you, just like severe pain.

He woke up with the impression that the shutter outside the bedroom window was banging as usual. Where had this strong wind suddenly come from?

He opened his eyes, turned on the light, and saw that the shutter was closed.

So what was banging? Then he heard the doorbell ring. Somebody was ringing and kicking the door. He looked at his watch. Ten past three. He got up and went to the door.

It was Fazio who'd been making all the racket.

"Forgive me, Chief, but I tried to ring you and there was no answer. Your phone must be unplugged."

"Has something happened?"

"Shaikiri was found dead."

In a way, he'd been expecting something like this.

"Wait while I go and get dressed."

He did it in the twinkling of an eye, and five minutes later he was sitting beside Fazio, who was at the wheel of a squad car.

"Tell me how he died."

"Chief, I don't know anything yet. It was Catarella who rang me. But the way he pronounced the name, Chaziki or something like that, it took me a good ten minutes to work out that he was talking about the Arab with the *Vanna*. And so, after trying unsuccessfully for a long time to phone you, I decided to come and get you."

"Do you at least know where we need to go?"

"Of course. To the jetty, to the *Vanna*'s berth."

On the quay, right in front of the yacht's gangplank, stood Lieutenant Garrufo, a sailor from the Harbour Office, and Captain Sperlì. Montalbano and Fazio shook hands with the group.

"What happened?" Montalbano asked Garrufo.

"Perhaps it's better to let the captain speak," said Garrufo.

"I was in my cabin," Sperlì began, "and about to get into bed, when I thought I heard a scream."

"What time was it?"

"Quarter past two; I looked instinctively at my watch."

"Where did it come from?"

"That's just it. It seemed to me to come from the crew's quarters. Which is on this side, the one closest to the quay."

"You heard a scream and nothing else? No other sound?"

"That was all. And the scream was sort of cut off, as though suddenly interrupted."

"And what did you do?"

"I left the cabin and went to the crew's quarters. Alvarez, Ricca, and Digiulio were sleeping soundly, but Shaikiri's bunk was empty."

"And so?"

"And so I said to myself that maybe the cry had come from the quay. So I went out on deck with a torch. But from what I could see by the light of the lampposts, the quay was deserted. I leaned out over the railing — the one right there, above the gangplank — and as I made that movement the torch pointed downwards. And that was when I saw him, completely by chance."

"Show me."

"You can see him from here, even without going on board."

He went to the edge of the quay and lit up the very narrow space between it and the side of the yacht. Montalbano and Fazio bent down to look.

There was a human body wedged vertically, head down, under water up to the bottom of the rib cage. Only the hips and absurdly spread legs remained out of the water.

A question immediately came to the inspector's mind.

"But with the body in that position, how could you tell it was Shaikiri?" he asked the captain.

Sperlì didn't hesitate for a second.

"From the colour of his jeans. He wore them often."

The jeans were so yellow they appeared to glow in the dark.

"Have you informed Mrs Giovannini?"

This time the captain was unable to hide an ever so brief moment of hesitation.

"N . . . no."

"Isn't she on board?"

"Yes, but . . . she's asleep. I'd rather not bother her. Anyway, what use would she be?"

"And have you told the crew?"

"Well, when they get drunk, it takes a while to wear off. And last night they must have had a lot to drink. It would only create confusion."

"Maybe you're right. I doubt they could tell us much. And what do you think happened, Captain?"

"What else? Poor Ahmed, drunk as he certainly must have been, probably took a wrong step and fell into the water, getting stuck with his head down. He must have drowned."

Montalbano made no comment.

"What should we do?" the lieutenant asked the inspector.

"If things went the way the captain says, then the case doesn't fall into my jurisdiction, but yours, Lieutenant. It looks like an accident that occurred within the precincts of the port. Don't you think?"

"I guess so," the lieutenant said reluctantly.

This time it would be his turn to stay up all night. As for Mrs Giovannini, she could forget about leaving any time soon.

158

★ ★ ★

As he was driving the inspector back to Marinella, Fazio asked him:

"Do you really think it was just an accident?"

Montalbano answered with another question.

"Can you explain to me why the captain felt the need to get a torch to go out and see if there was anyone on the quay? The quay is lit up, isn't it?"

"Of course. So why'd he take it?"

"So he could feed us that rubbish about how he happened to find the corpse, that's why. No torch, no way he notices the body."

"So you don't think it was an accident."

"I'm convinced it wasn't."

Fazio was confused.

"Then why didn't you —"

"Because it's better this way, I tell you. We'll let him believe we've swallowed his story. The body's going to end up in Pasquano's hands anyway. And tomorrow I'll give the doctor a ring."

When he got undressed again, it was almost five o'clock. But he no longer felt the least bit sleepy.

He prepared a pot of coffee, drank a mug of it, and sat down at the kitchen table with a sheet of paper and a biro.

He started wondering how the killers had managed to discover that the poor Arab was a sort of fifth-columnist in their midst. Maybe he had done something stupid. Like getting himself arrested twice.

As he was thinking, his hand started tracing lines randomly on the paper.

When he looked down, he realized he'd tried to sketch a portrait of Laura.

But since he didn't know how to draw, the portrait looked as if it had been done by an abysmal imitator of Picasso in a moment of total drunkenness.

At six o'clock, despite all the coffee he'd drunk, an irresistible need to sleep came over him. He went and lay down, slept three hours, and woke up to the sound of clatter in the kitchen.

"Adelina?"

"Ah, you's aweck? I bring you coffee now."

As he was drinking it, he asked her: "How are you feeling? Is the headache gone?"

"Yes, iss much better."

Thank God for Adelina's headache! If not for the fact that his housekeeper hadn't made him anything to eat for dinner, he wouldn't have dined at Enzo's, would not have gone for a walk along the jetty, and would not have run into Laura.

He left the house around ten o'clock. As soon as he had sat down in his office, he phoned Pasquano.

"The doctor's busy and doesn't want —"

"Listen, could you give him a message from me?"

"Of course."

"Tell him the mountain needs Mohammed."

The switchboard operator balked.

"But . . . but . . ."

The inspector hung up. And the very next second Mimì Augello came in. He looked a bit haggard.

"Busy night, eh, Mimì?" Montalbano said sarcastically.

"Leave me alone."

"So it went badly?"

"In a sense . . ."

"So she said no?"

"Are you kidding?"

"So tell me, then!"

"Look, Salvo, before I start talking, I need a double coffee. I sent Catarella to get some."

"And a nice zabaglione to give you strength, no? You look a little worn out to me."

Augello didn't reply. He just sat there in silence, waiting for Catarella to return.

He spoke only after he'd drunk the coffee, as promised.

"Last night, as I think I mentioned to you on the phone, I took Livia out to dinner."

Montalbano, who at that moment was lost in thoughts of Laura, leapt out of his chair.

"You did what to Livia?!"

"Salvo, have you forgotten that Mrs Giovannini has the same first name? Relax, it wasn't your Livia. So, anyway, I took her to a restaurant in Montelusa. She ate heartily and downed a bottle and a half of wine. Am I going to be reimbursed for expenses?"

"Weren't you reimbursed in kind? Go on."

"Well, on the way back, she took the initiative."

"How?"

"Listen, I'd rather skip the details."

"Just tell me how it started. What did she say?"

"What did she say? She didn't say a word!"

"Then what did she do?"

"We'd been in the car barely five minutes when she put her hand you know where."

So romantic, La Giovannini!

"And then she asked me where I intended to take her. I replied that, if she liked, we could go to my place, but she said she would feel more comfortable in her cabin."

"What time was it?"

"I didn't look at my watch, but it must have been past midnight. So we went on board and the minute we were below decks we ran into the captain."

"But they say he's La Giovannini's lover! Did he get upset? Angry? Did he say anything?"

"Not a word. He politely wished us goodnight and went up on deck."

"Maybe they're lovers in the sense that La Giovannini turns to him when she hasn't got anybody else."

"Maybe. At any rate, he didn't make a scene. So, the minute we went into her cabin, Livia took off all her clothes and —"

"Would you do me a favour, Mimì?"

"Of course."

"Don't call her Livia."

"Why not?"

"It makes me feel weird."

"All right, then. So, anyway, she got right down to business. And never stopped. Believe me, she's not a woman but a mincer that's always plugged in. Maybe that's why the captain grinned at me when he saw me with her. I was sparing him a night of forced labour! Luckily, around two-thirty, we heard that something serious had happened."

"What do you mean, 'luckily'?"

"I mean that she pulled the plug, even if only for a little while."

"*Mors tua vita mea*, in short."

"I'm sorry, Salvo, but that's really the way it is."

"So you heard a scream."

"A scream? There weren't any screams."

"What did you hear, then?"

"We heard the captain talking loudly on the telephone, saying that there'd been an accident."

"And then what?"

"Then Liv — I mean La Giovannini — got up, put on a dressing gown, and left the cabin. When she got back she said it was nothing serious. One of the crew had got drunk and fallen into the water, but they'd fished him back out."

"But do you know that in fact the man died?"

"Of course, I found that out later. She'd told me a different story."

"And why'd she do that?"

"Why? Because she wanted to grind the pestle in the mortar some more! She was afraid that if I found out that he was not only dead but stuck right there, just a few yards away from us, I wouldn't feel like doing it any more."

"When were you able to leave the yacht?"

"Around six-thirty this morning, after they took the body away. I went home, dozed a bit, and now here I am. I'm going to go and get some more sleep in a little while, because tonight, Liv — La Giovannini wants a second round."

"Were you able to talk to her during any lulls in the action?"

"Yes. At one point she wanted to know how much I earned, and so I came up with a figure a little higher than what our government hands out."

"Did she comment?"

"No. She wanted to know if I was married and whether I had any children. I said no. It's a good thing we didn't go to my house! She would have immediately noticed Salvuzzo's toys all over the place."

"They seem like perfectly normal questions."

"Yes, except that I was convinced they were asked with a specific purpose in mind. And so I told her I was unhappy at my job, and if I could find another I would be so much happier and grateful to anyone who gave me the chance . . . In short, I let her know I was available. I think she's already percolating something in her head."

"Listen, so how did you make out on the boat?"

"Not too badly, if I may say so myself. I think I was up to the task."

"I wasn't referring to the excellence of your performance in bed, about which I haven't the slightest

164

doubt, but to the fact that you didn't get to have your lesson in boat fuels with Lieutenant Belladonna."

"Ah, so you heard? But we were still able to have the lesson. It was all very quick, there wasn't much time."

A rafter falling on his head would have stunned the inspector less.

"Wh . . . when? Wh . . . where?"

"The poor thing! After being on her feet all night she phoned me at six in the morning."

"And she c-came to y-your place?"

"Salvo, what's got into you? Have you become a stutterer? No, she had me come to the Harbour Office."

Ding dong bell, ding dong bell.

"My dear Mimì," he said, standing up suddenly and going over and putting his arms around Augello. "Now go and get some rest, so you'll be strong for tonight."

Fazio, who was just coming in, stopped dead. What was happening to the inspector to make him go around embracing everybody?

"What do you want?" Montalbano asked him after Augello had left.

"I've come to remind you about calling Dr Pasquano."

"I've already called him, you know. What do you think, that I've got so old I'm starting to forget things?"

"What are you talking about, Chief? I didn't —"

"Look what I can still do."

And the inspector hopped up, feet together, onto the desktop.

"Upsy daisy!"

Fazio just looked at him, eyes popping out of his head. No doubt about it, the inspector needed to see a doctor.

"Ahh, Chief! 'At'd be Dacter Pasquino who —"

"Lemme talk to him."

"The phones are out of order here, Montalbano. All service has been interrupted."

"So where are you calling from?"

"I'm calling from a dreadful mobile. But don't keep me on this gadget for long. What does Mohammed want?"

"Today you were brought a sailor who'd fallen —"

"I worked on him early this morning."

"Want to tell me about it?"

"Not on a mobile. If you can be here in half an hour, I'll wait for you."

CHAPTER
THIRTEEN

Halfway between Vigàta and Montelusa there were two large trucks stopped along the road, one pointing in one direction, the other pointing in the other, so that both lanes, which were rather narrow, were blocked. The only vehicles that managed to pass through were scooters and motorcycles.

The truck drivers must have been old friends who hadn't seen each other for a long time. They'd got out of their cabs and were chatting blithely and laughing, slapping each other on the shoulders from time to time and not giving a damn about blocking the traffic. Behind Montalbano, who happened to be right behind the truck pointed towards Montelusa, a long queue of horn-blasting cars had formed.

At any other time Montalbano would have raised hell himself, honking the horn and yelling obscenities, and he would have ended up getting out of the car, spoiling for a fight. Instead he just sat there, a doltish smile on his face, waiting for the drivers to finish at their convenience and leave.

Ding dong bell.

And why was Dr Pasquano also in a good mood?

After greeting him, the doctor had shown him into his office without uttering a single nasty word or insult as he normally did. He must have won at poker the night before at the club.

But was the doctor really in a good mood, or was that just how it seemed to him, given the fact that everything he saw now seemed enveloped in a sort of halo of candied pink?

"So you want to know about the sailor? And why's that?"

"What do you mean, 'Why's that?' It's my job."

"But aren't you losing your edge with age?"

The inspector ignored this first provocation. He had to be patient and pretend not to have heard, because other, even more stinging insults would surely follow.

"Can you tell me your thoughts?"

"To all appearances, an accident."

"Oh, no you don't, Doctor! I'm not going to let you play cat and mouse with me. You can't say 'to all appearances'; you have to tell me what you know for certain."

"Why?"

"Because I don't think the work you do is based on hypotheses, clues, conjectures, and vague stuff like that . . ."

"Is that what you think of us? But aren't you aware that there is nothing in the world vaguer than man? And that we, too, proceed by means of conjecture? Do you think we're like a bunch of little popes who never make a mistake?"

"Doctor, I didn't come here to discuss the limitations of medical science. If you can't tell me anything certain, tell me something half-certain."

Pasquano seemed persuaded.

"I'll start with a question. Do you smell a rat in this whole affair?"

"Frankly, yes."

"Are you aware that when someone drowns we normally find a great deal of water in the lungs?"

"Yes, I know. But he didn't have any."

"Who said that? He had plenty of water."

"So then he drowned."

"But why do you have this bad habit of always jumping to conclusions? Hasn't old age made you a little more cautious?"

All this talk of old age was starting to get on the inspector's nerves.

"Doctor, get to the point. Did he have water in his lungs or not?"

"Don't get pissed off, mind you, or I'll clam up and say no more. There was water there, but not enough to drown him."

"So how did he die, then?"

"From a powerful blow to the nape of the neck, which killed him instantly. An iron bar. It fits."

"Fits with what?"

"With a sort of iron hook I noticed sticking out from the quay about a foot and a half above the water. You hadn't noticed it?"

"Doctor, when I looked, the hook was covered up by the body."

"Let me try to explain this a little better. The poor guy, drunk as he was — and he'd had a lot to drink — took a wrong step, fell into the narrow space between the quay and the side of the yacht, smashed his head against the hook, and died."

"Doctor, now I'm completely confused."

"That's natural, given your —"

"What killed him, the hook or the iron bar?"

"The fact that you don't understand is clearly owing to your age and not to any lack of clarity in my explanation. What I'm saying is that the killers were very clever. They're trying to make us believe he died when his head struck the hook. But the hook was green with sea moss. Whereas there was no trace of moss around the man's wound."

"And how do you explain the water in the lungs?"

"A precautionary measure."

"I don't understand."

"Don't you see what kind of shape you're in? Why don't you retire? Can't you see for yourself your time is up? Here is what happened, in my opinion. The killers — because there were at least two of them — grab him and push his head into the water to the point where he almost drowns and —"

"But the quay is high!"

"What makes you think they killed him there?"

"Where, then?"

"On the boat, of course! They take him on board, shove his head into a basin or something like that full of water, let him have a good drink, then pull him back out, choking his guts out, deal him the fatal blow, take him to the appointed place, and chuck him into the water from the quay."

"I still don't understand why you called it a precautionary measure."

"Do you see how seriously impaired your brain is? It was to make it look like he lived after the blow, in the few moments he had left of life."

There wasn't anything else to be learned here. On top of that, Montalbano couldn't stand the bastard's provocations any longer.

"Thank you, Doctor. I'm sorry, but have you informed the commissioner's office of the results of your postmortem?"

"Of course. I did my duty as soon as I'd finished my work."

If Dr Pasquano's reasoning was correct, and it did seem to make a great deal of sense, then the killing, with all the commotion of shoving the man's head repeatedly into a basin of sea water, could not have taken place on board the yacht.

Mimì Augello, however involved he was in bedroom gymnastics with La Giovannini at that moment, might have heard something. No, the risk would have been too great.

It's possible they did, at first, intend to carry out the killing on the yacht, but when La Giovannini appeared with Mimì on her arm, they would have been forced to change their plans.

Thus, when Captain Sperlì, while waiting for Shaikiri to return, saw Augello come on board, his only course of action would have been to race over to the *Ace of Hearts* and tell them of the hitch in their plans.

But there was no escaping it: if the killing did not take place on the yacht, it could only have occurred on the cruiser. Definitely not on the quay — or, at least, only the last phase could have taken place on the quay: moving the corpse and then chucking it into the water.

And this brought up something very important for the investigation: namely, that there was some sort of amorous correspondence between the *Vanna* and the *Ace of Hearts*. No question but that there were strong elective affinities between the two boats. In less literary terms, they must have been complicit in affairs so shady as to lead to murder.

If that was how it was, however, it implied something unexpected: that La Giovannini was completely in the dark as to the premeditated killing. Otherwise she would not have taken Mimì back to her cabin but gone to his place instead.

Was La Giovannini therefore innocent?

Wait a second, Montalbà. Try, as Pasquano warned, not to jump to conclusions.

Indeed, one could even hypothesize the exact opposite on the basis of the fact that La Giovannini brought Mimì on board. While they're dining in Montelusa, the lady gets an idea for creating an iron-clad alibi. She'll be rolling in the hay when the killing takes place.

No, that won't work.

It won't work because the alibi would be stronger if she went to Mimì's place.

172

And so?

Maybe La Giovannini didn't want the Arab to be liquidated on board her yacht. Maybe she wasn't opposed to killing him, but wanted to be left out of it, one way or another. Mimì's dinner invitation therefore came at just the right time, providing her with a unique opportunity.

By bringing him into her cabin, she forced all the others to change their plan.

Mimì said they had run into the captain in the mess room purely by chance. But that meant nothing. If they hadn't crossed paths with him, La Giovannini would probably have gone to talk to him, coming up with whatever excuse she could think of, so she could let him know that an outsider would be spending the night with her.

He went into his office, locked the door behind him, and rang Laura on the outside line.

As he was dialling, his heart started beating so wildly he was afraid he might be having a heart attack. How could he possibly be reduced to such a state at his age, like some adolescent in love for the first time?

"Hi. How are you?" he asked, his throat dry.

"Fine. And you?"

"I'm great. I wanted to tell you . . ."

Damn! He'd prepared a little speech that had worked like a charm in his head, but as soon as he'd heard her voice it had all vanished.

"What is it?"

"Well, I was about to go out to lunch, and was wondering . . ."

He got stuck, unable to speak. She came running to his assistance.

"If I could come out with you? I really wish I could, but I can't leave the office. I've got some stuff to do. But we could . . ."

"Yes?"

". . . see each other this evening, if you feel like it."

"Of . . . of course I feel like it. Where?"

"I'll come to your place and we can decide."

Why, suddenly, was she no longer uncertain? Why, suddenly . . . No, no more questions. Enjoy the sound of the bells. Ding dang dong, ding dang dong.

At Enzo's he gorged himself without restraint.

Apparently love whetted his appetite. Therefore a stroll along the jetty became a question of life or death.

He took the roundabout way, and as soon as he was within sight of the *Vanna* he realized with utter horror that the *Ace of Hearts* was not at its berth. It was gone, and there was no sign of it anywhere in the harbour.

Now a heart attack became a real possibility.

Matre santa! The boat had left, and it hadn't even grazed the inspector's consciousness that the *Ace of Hearts* could come and go as it pleased, since, officially at least, its owners had no connection to the murder.

He ran back to his car and left. Entering the station, he dashed past a startled Catarella and yelled: "Get me Lieutenant Belladonna at the Harbour Office on the line!"

174

"She's not a liutinnint, Chief."

"No? Then what is she?"

"A woman."

He couldn't waste any time on Catarella and continued into his office. He'd barely sat down when the call went through.

"What is it, Salvo?"

The sound of her voice sent him reeling, as usual. But he made an effort and pulled himself together.

"Sorry to disturb you, Laura, but it's important. As far as you know, has the *Ace of Hearts* sailed?"

"Not according to our information."

"But it's not in its berth."

"That's because they're still doing checks on the engines. They're probably doing some test runs out at sea."

He heaved a sigh of relief. "Do they have to tell you before they leave?"

"Of course. But why are you —"

"I'll tell you later. See you in a bit."

At just after four o'clock a call came from Augello.

"I need to speak to you urgently."

"Then come here."

"To the office? Not on your life! I don't want anyone to see me going into or coming out of the police station."

"You're right."

"What should we do?"

"Shall we say at my place in half an hour?"

"All right."

Walking by Catarella's cupboard, he said:

"I'm going out for about an hour. If Lieutenant Belladonna happens to call for me, tell her to ring me on the mobile phone. Can I rest easy on this?"

"You can rest easy as pie, Chief."

That way, if Laura called him because of some hitch in their plans, she would know how to reach him.

Mimi was punctual. "I've just had lunch with Liv — I mean La Giovannini."

"Where?"

"That was the first new twist. We'd agreed to meet this evening for dinner, but then she called me on the mobile to ask me if I wanted to come for lunch on the boat. I was still half asleep and needed more rest . . ."

"The rest of the warrior," Montalbano commented.

But Augello was in no mood for sarcasm.

"What choice did I have?" he said.

"None. You had to go."

"Indeed, and so I went. And I discovered the second new twist. Captain Sperli was going to eat with us."

"Strange."

"Not really. Wait. I realized she wanted to make me an official offer, and that's why the captain was there."

"In what capacity?"

"I dunno. Maybe as a witness, or partner, who knows."

"What was the offer?"

"She said she'd given a lot of thought to the things I'd said when I told her I wasn't happy in my current job, and she said she'd perhaps found a solution. But first I have to tell you something I forgot to mention this morning."

"What?"

"When she asked me how much I earned I tossed out a figure, but I also made it clear that I was topping it up."

"How?"

"By tampering with the gauge of the fuel's distribution valve."

"I see. So your credentials included a certain inclination for dishonesty."

"Exactly. She suggested I work for her, looking after some of her interests."

"So she's ready to entrust her concerns to someone who openly declares his dishonesty. It's a good thing to know. And what would these interests be?"

"She didn't specify. She said she would fill me in on everything in due course, if I accepted. She did, however, tell me something straight off. That I had twenty-four hours to accept or refuse. She wants to leave within three days at the very most, as soon as Shaikiri is buried."

"Shit!"

"And she added another thing, too. She said this work she was offering me would involve, to all intents and purposes, a move to a foreign country."

"Which?"

"South Africa."

"To a town called Alexanderbaai?"

Augello looked confused.

"What was that?"

"Never mind, for now. And how much are they going to give you?"

"They said my monthly pay will far exceed my expectations."

"And what did Captain Sperlì do the whole time?"

"He just sat there, quiet as a fish. What should I do?"

"The second round's on for tonight?"

"Yes, dammit."

"Listen, tell her you accept."

"Why?"

"Because that'll make her feel more secure. Try to find out about her interests in South Africa and exactly what sort of work she does. So how'd the business of the fuel end up?"

"I told her I was having the fuel analysed and would give her an answer tomorrow morning."

"Mimì, I have to ask you something about the night you spent with La Giovannini."

"I've already told you I don't feel like going into the details."

"I'm not interested in the erotic details. You said you realized something had happened when you heard Sperlì talking on the phone. Is that right?"

"Exactly."

"And what about before that? Did you hear anything that might have sounded like a body being dragged along, or cries of pain . . ."

"Absolutely not."

"Are you sure? Maybe you were too busy to —"

"Salvo, the walls in the boat are paper-thin! And you know what? I had to keep my hand over Livi — I mean

178

La Giovannini's mouth, or the whole crew would have heard her!"

Left by himself, he didn't feel like going back to the station.

"Catarella? Listen, I'm going to stay home for the rest of the day. If any important calls come in, from, say, Lieutenant Belladonna, tell them to call me here. Understand?"

"Poifectly, Chief."

He noticed that the floor of the veranda looked dirty. For reasons entirely impenetrable to him, Adelina, who kept the house sparkling clean, considered the veranda off-limits and never bothered with it. This suddenly seemed unacceptable, perhaps because Laura would soon be there. Grabbing a broom from the cupboard, he swept the tiles and then scrubbed them hard until they began to shine.

Then he went and opened the fridge. Seafood salad. On to the oven: pasta with broccoli and mullet in saffron sauce. He would leave it up to Laura to decide whether they should eat in or go out.

He went and had a hot shower to try to calm his nerves. He changed into clean underwear and clothes.

Choosing a book, he went and sat on the veranda and began reading. But he couldn't understand a word, because with each new line he'd already forgotten what he'd read in the one before.

At last, at a quarter to eight, the telephone rang.

"Laura, so, when are you coming?"

"This is Commissioner Bonetti-Alderighi," said Bonetti-Alderighi, sounding as Bonetti-Alderighi as humanly possible.

CHAPTER
FOURTEEN

His heart sank.

It was hopeless: if Mr Commissioner was annoying the inspector at home, at that hour, then the problem must be very, very serious. And it would make him lose time and, as a result, miss his date with Laura.

The horizon went from being cloudless to darkening by the second. He was lost.

"Montalbano! What, aren't you going to reply?"

"I'm right here, Mr Commissioner."

"I called your office."

Meaningful pause.

"So?"

"And they told me you'd gone home several hours ago!" said the commissioner, emphasizing the last three words with a rising tone.

Was he reproaching the inspector for being a lay-about, a shirker, a treacherous scrounger? Montalbano became incensed.

"Mr Commissioner, I am not a loafer! I —"

"That's not what I'm calling about."

Ah, you see? It really was a serious matter! Better not fly off the handle. Take it easy.

"Then what can I do for you?"

"I want to see you immediately!"

Shit! Take your time, Montalbà.

"Where?"

"What kind of question is that? Here, now!"

"Where, in your office?"

"Where do you think? In a bar?"

"Now?"

"Now!"

But Laura would be arriving in a few minutes!

If the commissioner thought he was going to drive to Montelusa, he had another think coming! They couldn't drag him away even in chains!

Montalbano assumed an apologetic tone.

"I really can't, believe me."

"And why not?"

He had to come up with a lie that would make it impossible for him to leave his house. He decided to throw in his lot with improvisation.

"Well, you see, when I got home I slipped and got a nasty sprained ankle which —"

"Which certainly won't prevent you from seeing a certain Laura!" Bonetti-Alderighi interrupted sarcastically.

Montalbano became incensed again.

"Aside from the fact that this Laura is a physiotherapist who is going to try to remedy the situation with massages — and you really have no idea just how desperately I am hoping she succeeds — you should know that if it were indeed the sort of encounter you are insinuating, a sprained ankle would hardly prevent me from —"

182

"So you really can't move?" Bonetti-Alderighi interrupted him, to stop him from getting lewd.

"No, I can't."

"What if I sent someone to pick you up?"

"I still don't think I could make it."

A brief pause for reflection on the commissioner's part.

"Well, then, I'll come to you."

"When?"

"Right now."

"Noooooooooo!"

A wolflike sort of howl had escaped his lips. He absolutely had to prevent the commissioner from coming, whatever the cost.

"Why are you yelling?"

"A shooting pain in my foot."

If he came to his house, he would certainly run into Laura. Who would even be in uniform. It would be hard to convince the commissioner that physiotherapists wore naval uniform. And things would turn nasty.

"No, don't bother, sir. You see . . . with a little effort I can try to get up and come to your office."

"I'll be waiting for you."

What was he going to do now?

First of all, he had to inform Laura. He rang the Harbour Office, but they told him she'd already left. He tried her mobile, but it was turned off.

He immediately called Gallo and told him to come and pick him up in a squad car.

Cursing the saints, he removed the shoe and sock from his left foot, went into the bathroom, wrapped half a roll of cotton around his ankle and then fixed this in place with an entire roll of gauze. He'd actually done a pretty good job of it; the whole area looked quite swollen from the sprain.

Then he grabbed a slipper, but the foot was too fat to fit. So he cut the slipper with a pair of scissors. Now the foot fitted, but the slipper was too loose and fell off with every step he took.

Desperate, he grabbed a roll of packing tape and wound this round and round his foot, slipper, and ankle.

To make his limp more convincing, he needed a cane. But he didn't own one, and so he rummaged through the utility cupboard and came up with a red plastic broomstick.

Now he looked exactly like a Sardinian shepherd from Campidano.

When Gallo saw him, his jaw dropped.

"Chief! What happened to you?"

"Don't give me any shit, just drive me to the commissioner's office."

His mood was so black that squid ink seemed grey by comparison. For the entire journey, Gallo didn't dare open his mouth.

Bonetti-Alderighi seemed not to notice the inspector's pastoral get-up. Though he didn't tell him to sit down, Montalbano did so anyway, groaning and sighing as if from a script.

The commissioner, however, heard none of it, or pretended not to.

Without a word he raised his right hand, index and middle finger extended and spread. Montalbano looked first at the fingers and then, questioningly, at the commissioner's angry face.

"Two," Bonetti-Alderighi then said.

"You want to play *morra*?" Montalbano asked with an angelic expression.

Would that he had never said it!

Bonetti-Alderighi's hand then closed in a fist, and the fist came crashing down on the desktop, nearly breaking it.

"Jesus Christ, Montalbano! You are stark, raving mad! Don't you realize that?"

"Realize what?"

"Two people have been murdered in Vigàta! And you . . ."

Choked with rage, the commissioner couldn't finish his sentence and ended up coughing.

He was forced to stand up, go and open the mini-fridge, and drink a glass of water.

When he sat down again, he seemed a little calmer.

"Do you admit that you knew the man found in the dinghy had been murdered?"

"Yes, and in fact —"

"Silence! Do you admit that you knew a North African sailor was also murdered?"

"I don't see why I shouldn't have —"

"Quiet! Do you or don't you admit that you then began to investigate the matter?"

"Of course. It was my duty to —"

"Shut up!"

Silence, quiet, and shut up. Montalbano began to admire the variety of the commissioner's injunctions. He wanted to see if Bonetti-Alderighi could come up with any others.

"Look, Mr Commissioner —"

"Button it! I'll do all the talking, for now."

Silence, quiet, shut up, and button it. He tried again.

"But I would like to —"

"Sshhh!" said the commissioner, bringing his index finger to his lips.

No, sshhh didn't count. It had to be verbal. But Montalbano didn't feel like playing any more and clammed up.

"Now I want you to answer a question I have for you, but without equivocating, without digressing, without —"

"Stalling, cavilling, changing the subject, beating around the bush?" Montalbano suggested in a rapid-fire burst to put any thesaurus to shame.

The commissioner looked at him, nonplussed.

"Are you mocking me?"

Montalbano assumed a demure expression.

"I wouldn't dare."

"Then cut the shit and answer!"

"May I make an observation?"

"No."

Montalbano fell silent.

"Answer!"

"If you won't let me make my observation . . ."

"All right, make your observation and then answer my question!"

186

"The observation is the following. I only wanted to point out, in all humility, that you forgot to ask your question."

"Ah, yes. You see? You are the only person here with the ability to make me so furious that I get all —"

"Confused? Distracted? Disoriented? Muddled?"

"Stop it, for Christ's sake! I don't need your stupid suggestions! At any rate, why didn't you deign to inform either the public prosecutor or me of these investigations? Can you tell me?"

"And how did you find out?"

"Don't ask idiotic questions! Just answer!"

With all his talking, he was making him miss his appointment with Laura. Montalbano decided to cut things short.

"I completely forgot."

"You forgot?" the commissioner repeated, dumbfounded.

Montalbano threw up his hands.

Bonetti-Alderighi turned red as a beetroot and emitted first a sort of roar and then an elephantine trumpet blast. It sounded like they were at the zoo.

"But what . . . exactly . . . do you think you're doing? Runn-running your own private inves-tigating firm?" the commissioner yelled, stammering in rage and standing up, index finger pointed at the inspector.

"No, but —"

"Silence!"

What? Was he going to restart, da capo, the aggravating litany of silence, quiet, and shut up? They wouldn't get out of there before dawn!

"And you listen to me, Montalbano," the commissioner continued. "As of this moment you are removed!"

"From what?"

"From the investigations. Inspector Mazzamore will handle them."

Never heard of him. Must be a new arrival. They changed every two weeks. Montelusa Central Police was a revolving door.

The only one who never left was pain-in-the-arse Bonetti-Alderighi.

Montalbano was about to object when he realized that this new development would allow him more time to devote to Laura.

"All right, then, if you don't mind, I'll remove myself," said Montalbano, anxious to leave. Leaning on the broomstick, he stood up, groaning and twisting his mouth as though in great pain.

The commissioner was unmoved.

"Where are you going?"

"Home to lie down, so —"

"Ha ha ha!" the commissioner laughed, sounding like Mephistopheles.

"Why are you laughing, may I ask?"

"You're not going home!"

Montalbano turned pale. For a brief moment he was afraid that Bonetti-Alderighi would have him arrested. The man was capable of it. But the commissioner continued:

"Now you are going to go into Dr Lattes's office — he's already waiting for you, in fact — and the two of you are going to reconstruct the list of the documents that were destroyed."

And since Montalbano, annihilated, could no longer move, the commissioner prodded him.

"Go on! Out with you!"

While crossing the waiting room, still limping to keep up appearances, Montalbano managed to curse all the saints in heaven.

Upon seeing him, Dr Lattes, without even noticing the Sardinian shepherd get-up, immediately asked him: "How's the little one?"

"He's dead," Montalbano answered mournfully.

With his balls already in a blinding spin, he'd be damned if he was going to keep the promise he'd made to Livia!

Lattes stood up, ran up to him, and embraced him.

"I'm so terribly sorry."

Maybe there was a way out. Montalbano buried his face in Lattes's shoulder and emitted a sobbing sound.

"And instead of being with my little boy . . . I have to be here and —"

"Good heavens, no!" said Lattes, hugging him even more tightly. "Go straight home! We'll talk about it some other time!"

It was all the inspector could do not to kiss his hand.

When he left Lattes's office it was already past ten. He dashed down the stairs, not bothering to wait for the lift, which was slow, and raced to the car.

"We're going to Marinella, quick!"

"Shall I turn on the siren?" asked Gallo, pleased.

"Yes."

Montalbano would have suffered less in a racing car on the track at Indianapolis. At one point it occurred to him that if he wasn't going to be handling the case any longer, there was no need for Mimì to engage in another night of gymnastics with La Giovannini. He might as well spare himself the effort.

He dialled Augello's mobile number.

"Montalbano here. Can you talk?"

"Ah, Gianfilippo! How good to hear from you!" said Augello. "Where are you calling from? Tell me, what can I do for you?"

In other words, he couldn't talk. Obviously La Giovannini was right beside him.

"I wanted to tell you that if you want to bail out, you can."

"Why?"

"Because the boss has decided to take me off the case. So it's not our concern any more."

"Listen, Gianfilippo, I don't think you can back out at this point, you know what I mean? It's too late. Once you're out on the dance floor, you have to dance. I'm sorry, but that's the way I see it. So you take care now, and we'll talk again tomorrow."

Which meant that his phone call had arrived past regulation playing time.

He immediately noticed that there was no sign of Laura's car in front of the house. He bade Gallo a hasty goodbye, opened the door, and went inside.

Laura wasn't on the veranda, either, like last time.

190

She hadn't waited for him. Or, more likely, she had waited for him but then became convinced he wasn't going to come any time soon and had left.

He went and stuck his head under the bathroom tap to cool his anger, then plucked up his courage and dialled her number.

"Hi, Salvo here."

"Yes?" she said cold as ice.

He had to stay calm and try to explain clearly what had happened.

"Forgive me, Laura, I'm truly sorry, but I got a call from the commissioner and —"

"I thought something had come up."

Then why was she so distant? "Listen, I'll tell you what we can do to set things right. Wait for me outside the front door of your building in fifteen minutes, and I'll come and pick you up."

"No." She'd said it without hesitation. A "no" as crisp and clean as a gunshot to the chest.

"It's not that late, you know," he insisted. "Have you already had dinner?"

"I don't feel hungry any more." Her voice sounded strange, neither indifferent nor angry. It was like a smooth barrier against which all words slid off, leaving no trace.

"Come on, once you sit down, your hunger will return."

"It's too late."

"All right, but I'll come anyway."

"No."

"We could at least spend half an hour together, no?"

"No."

"What's wrong? Are you upset? You know, I did call you at the Harbour Office to tell you I was running late, then I tried your mobile phone, but I —"

"I'm not upset."

"All right, then. Shall we meet tomorrow?"

"I don't think so."

"Why not?"

"Because I've been thinking about this, and I've come to the conclusion that the commissioner's phone call was providential."

There was no way any phone call from Bonetti-Alderighi could ever be providential. It would be against nature. "What do you mean?"

"I mean that it was fate. It was a very precise sign."

Was she raving? "Listen, explain yourself a little better."

"It means there can never be and must never be anything between us."

"Don't tell me you believe that sort of foolishness!" She didn't reply, and Montalbano got further incensed. "What, do you get up and first thing every morning read the horoscope in the paper?"

Laura hung up.

Montalbano redialled the number, but the phone rang and rang without reply.

His appetite, naturally, had gone south.

The only thing to do was to sit out on the veranda, armed with cigarettes and whisky, and wait for the rage to subside so he could go to bed.

Wait a second, Montalbà. Don't you think it's a little strange that the only emotion you're feeling at this moment is rage? And not regret or sadness?

And if I feel only rage, does that mean something?

Yes, sir, it certainly does. Shall we postpone the discussion until after you've ascertained that you have enough cigarettes and whisky in the house?

He went out, ducked into the Marinella Bar, came back, and as he was about to unlock the door, he heard the phone ringing. In his haste, he fumbled with the keys and had to put the bottle down to open the door.

Naturally, by the time he raised the receiver, he heard only a dial tone.

How was it possible he could never manage to pick up the phone in time?

It must certainly have been Laura trying to call.

So, what to do now? Call her himself? And what if it hadn't been Laura? At that moment the phone started ringing again.

"Laura!"

At the other end, total silence. Want to bet it was that pig-headed commissioner again?

"Who is this?" the inspector asked.

"Livia."

In an instant, he was bathed in sweat.

"And I want to know who this Laura is," she added.

Not knowing in his despair what to say, he laughed.

"Ha ha!"

"You find my question funny?"

"So you're jealous, eh?"

"Of course I'm jealous. Answer me and stop acting like an imbecile."

She'd said it in exactly the same tone of voice as Bonetti-Alderighi.

"You're not going to believe me, but when you called, I was trying to think of the name of Petrarch's beloved, and it finally came to me as I was picking up the receiver . . ."

"And you think I'm so stupid as to swallow that explanation?"

By now Montalbano's sweat was pouring into his eyes, blinding him, while the receiver was slipping out of his hand.

"I'm sorry, could I call you back in five minutes?"

"No," said Livia, hanging up.

CHAPTER
FIFTEEN

The phone call from Livia was really the last thing he needed. Sighing sadly, he picked up the bottle on the ground outside the door, put it down on the table on the veranda, went and washed his face, and finally sat down outside.

What was it he was supposed to think about?

Ah, yes, the reason why he felt only rage, instead of regret or sadness.

But is it really so necessary to tackle this question right now? When your head is in such a state of confusion? Couldn't you postpone it?

No, I really think this is the right moment. And I don't want to hear any childish excuses. So, buck up, and proceed. In what circumstances does a person feel rage? Answer me.

Well, there could be any number of reasons for —

No, no, stop beating around the bush, stop equivocating, as the commissioner might say. Stick to the subject at hand. The question couldn't be clearer: why did you become enraged when Laura refused to see you?

Well, because I really wanted to see her and —

Are you really so sure?

Of course.

No, you're lying to yourself. You're like the person who cheats when he plays solitaire.

Then why?

I'll tell you why. Quite simply because you were unable to do what you wanted to do.

No, when you put it that way, you make it sound vulgar. As if I wanted only to —

Oh, yeah? Wasn't that your intention?

Come on, cut the bullshit!

What bullshit? Listen, if you truly loved her, at this moment you would be sorrowful, forlorn, call it whatever you like, but not angry.

Explain what you mean.

If you're angry, it means what you really feel for Laura is not love. Rage, in fact, means you consider Laura an object you want to grab, something that manages to elude your grasp at the last minute.

Are you saying I see her as an . . . a . . .

Let's say a fish. Which you want to catch with a landing-net. You manage to get the fish to go into the net, but as you're lifting it out of the water, the fish wiggles out, breaks free, and dives back into the water. And you're left there like an idiot, with an empty net in your hand. And that's why you feel enraged.

So what would you call what I feel for her?

Attraction. Desire. Vanity. Or else you see her as a kind of raft you desperately want to grab hold of to avoid drowning in the seas of old age.

So it's not love?

No. And you know what I say to you? That if you really were seriously in love with her, you would try and understand her motives and misgivings.

He went on this way for another two hours. When he'd finally emptied the bottle, he laid his head down on his folded arms on the table and fell into a sort of troubled half-sleep.

The cool dawn air woke him.

He stood up, went into the house, had a nice hot shower, shaved, and drank his customary mugful of espresso.

There was only one question rattling around in his brain: would he be able to stand never seeing Laura again? Would he have the strength?

He came to the conclusion that he would respect her feelings, would not force her, and would not take any initiatives himself.

But at that moment, he had to find a way to pass the hours until it was time to go to the office. He grabbed Petrarch's *Canzoniere* and decided to read it in the early morning light.

He read for a long time, but at one point he came to a poem that said:

My ship sails brimful of oblivion
O'er harsh seas on a winter's night
Between Scylla and Charybdis . . .

and he had to stop. He had a lump in his throat.

Wasn't he, too, caught in a sort of sea storm between Scylla and Charybdis?

He closed the book, looked at his watch. It was seven o'clock.

At that moment the doorbell rang. Who could it be, so early in the morning? For a split second he hoped it was Laura dropping by before going on duty. He went and opened the door. It was Mimì Augello.

Sleepy, wasted, and unshaven.

"How are you feeling, Mimì?"

"Ground to a pulp."

His first question was: "Could I have some coffee?"

The second question was: "Could I have a shower?"

And the third, and last, was: "Could I use your razor?"

Finally, clean and refreshed, and sitting down on the veranda, he began to tell his story.

"When you called me last night, I was already on board and had no excuse for leaving. Why did you do it?"

"Do what?"

"Phone me."

"To spare you from spending another night with her."

"I don't believe you."

"Then why, in your opinion?"

"Because you felt guilty."

"Guilty towards you? Ha ha ha! That's a good one!"

"Not towards me, but towards Beba. I realized why, in fact, you called me. You felt guilty for sending me off to sleep with Liv — La Giovannini."

As Mimì was talking, Montalbano realized that he was right. In reality, he hadn't explicitly thought of Beba,

198

but had made the phone call on impulse, without really knowing why. He'd simply acted. Good for Mimì, then! He was right on the money. But the inspector didn't feel like granting him the satisfaction of knowing this.

"I never actually told you to sleep with her," he said.

"Oh, no? Well, you're a fine hypocrite! She's the kind of woman — and you knew this from the start — who doesn't give a shit about moonlight strolls by the sea! You didn't actually say it, but you implied it. But I think we'd better just drop it. Do you still want to know what happened?"

"Of course."

"But the commissioner took you off the case!"

"Tell me just the same."

"We had dinner on board."

"Sorry to interrupt you, but did you two talk at all about Shaikiri?"

"Just a brief mention. La Giovannini told the captain —"

"Did he eat with you?"

"Yes, but if you interrupt me every —"

"Sorry."

"She told the captain to ask for the body to be returned so they could bury it and then leave. So, to continue. Your phone call came too late because, among other things, I'd already told Livia and Sperlì that I'd agreed to come and work with them."

"Did they explain any better what the work would involve?"

"Only one thing seemed clear to me. Livia told me she'd given a lot of thought to how they could use me, and had decided that instead of having South Africa as my base, it was better if they sent me to Freetown."

"Where's that?"

"In Sierra Leone. I told her it didn't make any difference to me, that what mattered most to me was to earn as much money as possible. And I made it quite clear that I was ready to close not one eye but both."

"But did she tell you what her interests were in those parts?"

"Yes, coffee and tobacco plantations, and a very large share in extractive concerns."

"Extractive concerns? And what does that mean?"

"Mining, I think."

"Find out anything else?"

"No. We're going to meet again at five this evening to work out the terms of the contract. Maybe they'll tell me more then. But what do you think? Should I go back on board or not? If the case is no longer ours . . ."

"Lemme think for a minute. And what happened during the night?"

"You want details about what Livia wanted me to do?"

"I told you not to call her Livia! No, I only want to know whether anything happened that —"

"Wait. Yes, something did happen. Around midnight the captain knocked on the cabin door. Luckily we were taking a break. Liv — Giovannini went to open the door, completely naked. They talked quietly for a minute, with him standing outside and her inside, and then she closed the door, went to the rather large safe she has in her cabin, opened it, took out a folder, put

200

on her dressing gown, and went out. I got up immediately and took a quick look at what was inside the safe, but without touching anything."

"And what was there?"

"A lot of money: euros, dollars, yen . . . And files and folders, all with titles. And five or six registers. And there was a big fat binder with the words Kimberley Process written on it."

"And what does that mean?"

"Dunno. Listen, what course should I take now?"

"Theoretically, you should bail out. Your back's no longer covered. If you go on board again, it'll be without authorization."

"But it would be a shame to leave the whole thing hanging."

"I agree. What do you want to do?"

"I'd like to go to the five o'clock meeting just the same. I'm certain they're going to tell me something that'll help us screw them."

"And how will you extract yourself afterwards? You can't just say, 'Look, I've changed my mind, I've decided not to come with you.'"

"Of course not! They'd kill me!"

"I've got it!" Montalbano said suddenly.

"You've got what?"

"I know how to get you out of there. The Shaikiri method."

"Meaning?"

"I'll arrest you!"

"Come on! I think it's a little early in the morning for you."

"Mimi, believe me, it's the only way. You'll call me when you're about to go on board the *Vanna*. Fazio and Gallo will pretend to be on duty at the port. If you have any important news, you'll blow your nose as you're descending the gangplank. A minute later you'll be in handcuffs. You'll react angrily, make a big row, so that everyone on the *Vanna* and the *Ace of Hearts* knows what's going on, and that way, you'll make your exit and tell me everything you've learned once you return to the station. If you don't blow your nose, it'll mean you have nothing new to tell us, and we won't arrest you. Got that? You look doubtful. What's wrong?"

"I hope I remember to bring a handkerchief. I always forget."

Augello left and Montalbano went over to his bookcase and pulled out the calendar-atlas he'd already looked at. His ignorance of geography was disgraceful, to the point where he was capable of mistaking the locations of the five continents.

The first thing he did was to see what it said about South Africa.

And immediately he came across Kimberley, which was where the biggest diamond deposits were located. So big, in fact, that the place had become a sort of national monument. There were also platinum mines, not to mention iron, cobalt, and a great many other things that the inspector knew nothing whatsoever about.

And they produced tobacco but not coffee.

The coffee plantations, for their part, were in Sierra Leone, along with other tobacco farms. And there were enough diamonds, cobalt, and other minerals for everyone to have a merry old time. Enough, that is, for a merry old time to be had by the owners of the mines, which all belonged to foreign companies, whereas, according to the calendar-atlas, the life expectancy for the native populations was thirty-seven years for males, and thirty-nine for females.

At any rate, what La Giovannini had told Augello matched up with this reality. But in the inspector's brain, an annoying sort of bell had started ringing. Hoping to make it stop, he reread everything from the beginning.

But this only made the bell start ringing louder, so loud, in fact, that he began worrying that something might be happening to his brain.

Then he realized that it was the telephone. At first he decided not to answer, but then he thought it might be Laura and started running.

"Chief, ya gotta 'scuse me fer 'sturbin' yiz at home in yer own home."

"What is it, Cat?"

"Dacter Micca called juss now."

Never heard of him. The only Micca he knew of was the famous Pietro, the Piedmontese soldier he'd read about in history books.

"Did he tell you his first name?"

"Yessir, Chief. 'Is firss name's Jerry."

"You mean as in Jerry Lewis?"

"Yessir, 'ass azackly right, Chief."

Jerry Micca. Geremicca!

"And what did he say?"

"'E axed yiz to go an' see 'im."

"Listen, Cat, since I have to go to Montelusa, you have to do me a favour."

"Yessir, Chief!"

The inspector was certain that Catarella had stood to attention when saying this.

"I want you to do an Internet search for the name Kimberley Process."

"No problem, Chief. Ya jess gotta tell me how iss writ."

"I'll try. The first letter is a K." A good three minutes passed without Catarella saying anything. Maybe he'd gone to look for a pen.

"Cat?"

"I'm here, Chief."

"Did you write down the K?"

"Not yet, Chief."

"Why not?"

"I's wunnerin' if iss a K witt or wittout the O."

"Without, Cat."

"So how you write a K wittout the O?"

At this rate, it was going to take them a week. Because once they got past the stumbling block of the K, there was still the Y at the end.

"Listen, Cat, tell you what. I'll write it down on a piece of paper and drop it off at the station for you before going to Montelusa, OK?"

As he was on his way to Vigàta, the inspector realized that Geremicca's call had come at absolutely the right moment. If he wanted to see Montalbano, then he must have received news from his French colleague, which meant that the investigation was about to be enriched with new elements, and the inspector could throw himself into it body and soul. He didn't give a flying fuck that the commissioner had taken him off the case; he would carry on just the same. The investigation was more vital to him than bread itself, and for one simple reason: it would not allow him any time to think about Laura.

He pulled up in front of the station, didn't bother to park, got out of the car, leaving the door wide open, went inside, gave the piece of paper with the name Kimberley Process written on it to Catarella, and said: "I'll be back in an hour."

"Wait, Chief."

"What is it?"

Catarella clearly felt awkward, as he kept looking at the tips of his shoes and opening and closing his hands in a fist.

"Well?" the inspector prodded him.

"Y'see, Chief, I gots somethin' I oughter tell yiz but I ain't 'ad the pleasure a tell yiz cuz I dunno whither I oughter tell yiz or no."

"All right, then, when you decide what's best, you can send me a telegram."

"Chief, this in't no jokin' matter!"

"Then out with it, for Christ's sake!"

"Please, Chief, le'ss go in yer office."

If this was Catarella's way of not wasting his time, well then . . . Catarella followed him down the hallway.

The door to the inspector's office was closed. Montalbano opened it and went inside.

Fazio was there, sitting in front of the desk with his back to them. Hearing someone come in, he turned around. At that moment the inspector noticed a funeral cushion of white flowers in the middle of his desk, the kind that one lays on coffins.

He turned pale, suddenly remembering the dream he'd had about his own funeral.

"What . . . what . . ."

He was unable to speak. He looked at Fazio, who was wearing a gloomy, worried expression.

"What else could it be, Chief? This is a classic Mafia warning."

It was true. Montalbano went over to the filing cabinet, on top of which he always kept a bottle of water, and drank a glass as his brain whirred at high speed.

There was only one explanation possible for this threat. The Mafia must definitely be involved in the activities of the *Vanna* and the *Ace of Hearts*. That flower cushion was meant to tell him that if he didn't back off, they would kill him. Never before had the Cuffaros or Sinagras gone to such lengths with him. Maybe the dream he'd had would even come true.

Montalbano said nothing. He batted the cushion with his hand in frustration, knocking it onto the floor.

"Catarella, get that thing and throw it in the bin."

Catarella bent down, picked up the cushion, and was about to leave the room when Montalbano asked him:

"When did they deliver it?"

"Juss five minutes afore ya got here."

"Did you see who brought it?"

"Yiss. Ciccino Pànzica, the floriss."

"Fazio, I want this Pànzica here in front of me in five minutes."

He had to admit it, he felt a bit scared. Normally he wouldn't, if not for that damned dream he'd had.

Ciccino Pànzica was about sixty years old, with skin as pink as a pig's.

"You must excuse me if I —"

"I'll ask the questions around here."

"Of course, sir."

"Who ordered that cushion from you?"

"They didn't say who they were. They ordered it over the phone."

Fazio intervened.

"How did you arrange for the payment?"

"They were going to send someone."

"And did this person come?"

"Yes, sir, yesterday evening."

"Would you recognize him if you saw him again?"

"If I saw him, yes. He was in uniform."

Montalbano and Fazio looked at each other, puzzled.

"What kind of uniform?" Fazio asked.

"Yours."

A Mafioso disguised as a policeman! This was becoming more and more troubling.

"Can I say something I wanted to say from the start?" the florist asked.

"Go ahead," said Montalbano.

"The policeman also gave me a little card, which I forgot to deliver with the cushion."

Normally, though, these kinds of threats never contained any written messages, Montalbano thought.

"Let's see it."

The florist handed it to him. It was a calling card in an envelope. Montalbano opened it. On the back of the card were the words: *Sincerest condolences. Lattes.*

CHAPTER
SIXTEEN

As Montalbano was entering Geremicca's office, he had no idea that in a few minutes, inside those four walls, a word would be uttered, only one, but that word alone would suffice to put him on the right track.

Upon seeing Montalbano, Geremicca stood up smiling and rotated his right hand in the air, as if to say that something really big had happened.

"Montalbano! You've landed a big one!"

"Me? What'd I do?"

"I emailed my French colleague a photocopy of the passport you gave me. And I told him that you'd told me that the name on the passport was the same as that of a character in a Simenon novel, if I remember correctly."

"That's right. And so?"

"And so he started telling me that a month ago they'd arrested an expert forger, a real master, but he refused to name his clients. They had, however, managed to confiscate among other things two passports ready for use. Your passport, together with these, made three. And thanks to the clue we'd given them, my friend discovered that the forger was in the

209

habit of using the names of characters from French literature. Imagine that!"

"I guess he liked to read."

"And there's more. The names the forger chose always had some connection with something the client did in real life."

"Can you give me a little more detail?"

"Sure. Just to give you an idea, my colleague said this Émile Lannec, the fictional character, owns a small steamship in the novel. Is that true?"

"Absolutely."

"Well, thanks to some other information, and despite the mangled face, my colleague was able to identify the man on the passport. His name is Jean-Pierre David. He has a clean record, but the police have had their eye on him for a while."

"And what's the thing connected to his real life?"

"His father used to own a small steamship, which eventually sank. And so the clue you gave them helped lead the French to the true identities of the other two whose passports were ready for use. They convey their heartfelt thanks to you."

"And why were they keeping an eye on this David?"

"Apparently he was part of a large organization involved in some heavy traffic."

"What kind of traffic?"

"Diamonds."

Montalbano gave a start. For a moment he couldn't see a thing. The lightning that had flashed through his brain was so bright, it had blinded him.

What to do next?

It should have been his duty to go at once, without wasting another minute, to the office of Mezzamore, no, Mozzamore, or whatever the hell his name was, and tell him point by point everything he had learned. Should have been, mind you. Because, according to the commissioner's orders, the inspector shouldn't even have gone to see Geremicca that morning. He should have told him, over the phone: "Thank you, my friend, but you should pass all information on to my colleague Mizzamore, since he's the one handling the case henceforth."

Instead, he'd gone. Thus committing an act of insubordination. Now if he went to Mozzamore and told him that the dead man had been identified, the commissioner could accuse him of insubordination or worse . . .

"But aren't you ashamed to be pulling out such lame excuses?" the voice of his conscience reproached him. *"The truth is you're such an egotist, such a selfish wretch that you don't want to share anything with anyone . . ."*

"Would you just let me think for a second?" Montalbano replied.

To report or not to report. That was the question.

In the end, his conscience won. He walked around the building, entered through the main door, and asked where Inspector Muzzamore's office was.

"You mean Mazzamore?" the person at the reception desk, who knew Montalbano, corrected him. "It's right next door to Dr Lattes's office."

Alas. Alas, alack, and wailaway. He had to proceed with extreme caution.

Instead of taking the lift, he climbed the stairs. When he'd reached the right floor, he stopped. There was a whole corridor to cross. He stuck his head out and saw none other than Lattes, standing right in the middle of the hallway, talking to someone.

No, he just couldn't go on any longer with this farce about the non-existent little boy who died.

He turned tail and left. He would give Mazzamore a ring. But later, whenever he happened to. There was no hurry.

"*Pretty good excuse you came up with there!*" his conscience needled him.

He told his conscience where to go, to the same place he probably too often sent it. Actually, there was no "probably" about it.

"Ahh, Chief, Chief! Ahh, Chief!"

Montalbano knew what this plaintive litany meant. "Did the commissioner call?"

"Yessir, 'e did, jess now, by tiliphone."

"What did he want?"

"'E said as how ya gotta go rilly rilly emergently t' see 'im, 'im being Mr C'mishner hisself."

Utterly and totally out of the question! No way could he risk running into Lattes. At the very least he would be forced to thank him for the funeral cushion.

"Tell Fazio to come to my office at once. And, by the way, did you find anything about the Kimberley Process?"

"Yessir, I did, Chief, I'll prinn it up straightaways."

Going into his office, the inspector noticed that one of the flowers that had come detached from the cushion when he'd knocked it to the floor had remained there. He bent down, picked it up, and threw it out of the window. He didn't want to see anything that might remind him of the dream he'd had of his funeral.

"What is it, Chief?" asked Fazio, coming in.

"You have to do me a favour. I want you to call the commissioner."

Fazio looked puzzled.

"Me?!"

"Why not? Do you find it offensive? Embarrassing?"

"No, Chief, but . . ."

"No buts. I want you to tell him a lie."

"About what?"

"He wants to see me right now, but for reasons of my own, I really can't go there just now."

"And what am I supposed to tell him?"

"Tell him that as I was driving to work somebody bumped into me, and you had to take me to accident and emergency and then home."

"Would you like to tell me, in case he asks, exactly what happened to you in the accident? Was it serious or minor?"

"Since I've already given him some other rubbish, just tell him I re-injured the same ankle I'd already sprained."

"And how did you get this sprain?"

"The same way I got bumped into."

"I see."

"And now I'd better get home fast, in case he phones me there."

"All right," said Fazio, turning to leave the room.

"Where are you going?"

"I'm going to my office to make the call."

"Can't you just do it here?"

"No, sir. I'm a better liar when I'm alone."

Fazio returned less than five minutes later.

"What did he say?"

"He said you've been having too many accidents lately and had better start taking better care of yourself."

"Didn't he believe it?"

"I don't think so. Chief, I think you'd better go home right away. He's definitely going to call."

"Did he say anything else?"

"Yes. He said you're going to have to resume the investigation because Inspector Mazzamore is too busy with another case."

"And you're telling me this now?"

"When was I supposed to tell you?"

"It should have been the first thing!"

They stood there for a moment in silence, staring at each other. "I'm not convinced," said Montalbano.

"Me neither. But it's not the first time he's given you back a case he'd taken away from you."

"I'm still not convinced. At any rate, I wanted to tell you that the body in the dinghy's been identified. His real name was Jean-Pierre David, and the French police had been keeping an eye on him."

"Why was that?"

"Apparently he was involved in diamond trafficking."

Fazio's eyes narrowed to little slits.

"Ah, so the people from the *Ace of Hearts* . . .?"

"Are up to their necks in this. Cross my heart and hope to die. We have to work out a way to set them up. And we've got to do it quickly, because they could leave at any moment. Oh, and one more thing."

"Tell me."

"I want you and Gallo to be ready. This afternoon, around five o'clock, there's something we have to do."

"What's it involve?"

"We'll probably have to arrest Mimì."

Fazio opened his mouth and then closed it again. He turned red in the face, and then pale as a ghost. He collapsed into a chair.

"Wh . . . Why?" he asked in a faint voice.

"I'll explain later."

At that moment Catarella came in with a few sheets of paper in his hand.

"I prinnit it all up, Chief."

Montalbano folded them and put them in his jacket pocket.

"See you later," he said.

And he headed home.

But how had the telephone acquired the fine habit of ringing just as he was coming through the door? Since he'd given up hope that it was Laura trying to reach him, he took his time.

He opened the French windows to the veranda, then went into the kitchen.

Since he would have to eat at home, he wanted to see what Adelina had made for him. He opened the oven.

And what a discovery it was. Pasta 'ncasciata and mullet *alla livornese*.

The telephone, which had stopped ringing, started again. This time he went and picked up.

It was the commissioner.

"Montalbano, how are you feeling?"

Just as Fazio had predicted, the bastard wanted to verify whether he had actually had an accident. And Montalbano was ready to oblige him. He began:

"Well, the crash wasn't —"

"I wasn't talking about that," the commissioner cut him off sharply.

Oh no? Then what did he want to talk about? Maybe it was best to keep quiet and see where he was headed.

"I was referring to your mental health, which I'm very worried about."

What was this? Was he telling him he thought he was going insane? How dare he?

"Listen, Mr Commissioner, sir, I can put up with a lot, but I will not tolerate any comments about my mental —"

"I'll do the talking here, Inspector. You just answer my questions."

"Listen, this isn't —"

"Dammit, Montalbano, that's enough!" Bonetti-Alderighi snapped.

He must really be angry. Better let him get it out of his system. But the question he asked was the last thing Montalbano expected.

"Is it true that you suffered a terrible loss a few days ago?"

The inspector felt annihilated. Dr Lattes must have told the commissioner that he'd lost his son!

"In other words, that a son of yours died?" the commissioner continued in a frosty tone of voice.

How the hell was he going to get out of this one?

"And your wife is in despair?"

The commissioner's voice was now well below zero.

"And can you explain to me how this can be when, as far as anyone knows, you have neither wife nor children?"

A polar ice floe.

What the hell to do now? A hundred possible replies raced through his mind at supersonic speed but he ruled them all out. None seemed convincing enough. He opened his mouth, but was unable to speak. The commissioner spoke instead.

"I understand," he said.

The frost attained by this point was only possible in laboratories.

"I do hope you'll one day let me know your reasons for playing such a mean, vulgar trick on a perfect gentleman like Dr Lattes."

"It wasn't a . . ." he finally managed to utter.

"I don't think one can talk about something so serious and base over the telephone. So let's stop trying, for now. Have you been informed that I had to turn the investigation back to you?"

"Yes."

"If it were up to me, you . . . but I was forced to do so, against my will . . . But let me be very clear about this. If you step out of line this time, I'll screw you. And you must keep me continually up to date on the progress of the case. Good day."

"Good night" would have been more appropriate.

Matre santa, how embarrassing! Enough to make one want to disappear underground! There was, however, a positive side to it: from now on Lattes would never again ask him for news of his family.

And the commissioner, in his rage, had let slip an important admission. Namely, that he'd been forced to give the case back to him, against his will. Therefore, someone else had intervened. Who could it have been? And, more importantly: why?

But since the commissioner had called, and it had not been possible to give any ready answers to his questions, the inspector decided to go out and eat at Enzo's.

As he was heading towards the port for his customary stroll, he had an idea. Maybe he could do something to help to loosen La Giovannini's tongue and make her reveal to Mimì exactly what she did while sailing the high seas, and perhaps confirm whether it was the sort of traffic he already suspected her of.

He took the roundabout way to the lighthouse, and when he was in front of the *Vanna*, he headed up the gangplank and stopped on the deck.

"Anybody here?"

Captain Sperlì answered from the mess room.

"Who's there?"

"Inspector Montalbano."

"Come in, come in."

The inspector went below through the hatch. The captain was finishing his lunch. Beside him stood Digiulio, serving as his waiter.

"Oh, I'm sorry," said Montalbano. "If you're eating, I can come back later."

"No, please, I've already finished. Would you have some coffee with me?"

"I'd love some."

"Please sit down."

"Mrs Giovannini's not here?"

"She's here but she's resting. If you like, I —"

"No, no, please let her sleep. I heard you were having some problems with your fuel. Has that been set right?"

"Apparently it was a false alarm."

"So you'll be leaving as soon as you can?"

"If we can get poor old Shaikiri's body back tomorrow morning, as we've been promised, we'll bury him and then set sail in the afternoon."

Digiulio brought the coffee. They drank it in silence. Montalbano then started digging in his pockets. To get better access to what he was looking for, he pulled out the sheets of paper Catarella had given him, and set these down on the table. On the top sheet were the words, in block letters: KIMBERLEY PROCESS. He hadn't yet had the time to read them, but whatever they said, they must nevertheless have a precise meaning for the captain, since Giovannini kept a file with the same name in her safe. And indeed, the moment the captain's eyes fell on the sheet of paper, he gave a start.

At last Montalbano extracted the pack of cigarettes from his pocket, lit one, and put the papers back in his pocket.

Meanwhile Sperlì had become visibly nervous.

"Look, if you'd like to speak to Mrs Giovannini, I can go —"

"I wouldn't dream of it!" said Montalbano, getting up. "It was nothing of importance. I'll pass by again later. Have a nice day."

He went up on deck, then back down onto the quay. Sperlì hadn't budged. He seemed to have turned to stone.

Perhaps he really ought to find out what this Kimberley Process was, the inspector thought, considering the effect it had on the captain.

But he would look into it later, at the office. First the walk to the lighthouse.

As he was sitting on the flat rock, all at once the thought of Laura assailed him with all the ferocity of a rabid dog. It caused him genuine, physical pain. The violence was perhaps due to the fact that he had managed for a while not to think of her, thanks to his preoccupation with the case. It had been his sort of revenge. But now her absence sliced right through him. It was an open wound.

No, he couldn't phone her. He mustn't. There was, however, one thing he could do that wouldn't have negative consequences.

He got in his car and headed to the Harbour Office.

Outside the entrance stood the usual guard and two sailors, chatting. He drove a little further past, then parked in such a way that he could see in the rear-view mirror who went in and out.

He stayed there for fifteen minutes, smoking one cigarette after another. Then, in a moment of lucidity, he felt embarrassed, ashamed of himself.

What was he doing there? He hadn't even done this sort of thing when he was sixteen, and now he was doing it at fifty-eight? Fifty-eight, Montalbà! Don't you forget it! Or was it perhaps the folly of old age that made him act this way?

Humiliated and depressed, he started the car and drove back to the station.

As soon as he sat down, he pulled out Catarella's printouts and was about to start reading them when the phone rang.

"Ah, Chief! 'At'd be Dacter Lattes onna line who —"

"I'm not here!" He yelled it so loudly that Catarella complained. "*Matre santa*, Chief! Ya got my ears a-ringin'!"

The inspector hung up. He didn't feel like talking. How could he ever justify his actions to Lattes? How could he ask to be forgiven? With what words? Why had he been so stupid as not to follow Livia's advice?

So, the Kimberley Process was . . .

The telephone rang again.

"'Scuse me, Chief, but there's a young lady says she wants a talk t'yiz poissonally in poi —"

"On the phone?"

"Nah, she's onna premisses."

He didn't have the time. He absolutely had to read those printouts.

"Tell her to come back tomorrow morning."

So, the Kimberley Process was . . .

Again the phone.

"Chief, ya gotta try 'n' unnastand but the young lady says iss rilly rilly urgentlike."

"Did she say what her name was?"

"Yessir. Vanna Digiulio."

CHAPTER
SEVENTEEN

To say he was astonished wouldn't have been accurate.
If anything, he felt a sort of small satisfaction for having
been right on target; indeed, he'd been certain the girl
would turn up sooner or later to explain the whole
affair to him. One thing, however, did indeed astonish
him no end: that Catarella, for the first time in his life,
had neither mangled nor mistaken her name.

For a second, upon seeing her, he thought that the
young woman standing before him was not the same
one he'd met. And that the whole business was even
murkier than he'd imagined. How many Vanna
Digiulios were there, anyway?

This one was blonde, without glasses, and had
beautiful blue eyes. More importantly, she didn't have
that beaten-dog look that had made him feel so sorry
for her. On the contrary, to judge by the way she
walked, she seemed like a decisive, self-assured person.

She smiled at Montalbano as she held out her hand.
Montalbano, standing erect, returned the greeting.

"I've been waiting for you," he said.

"I knew you would be," she said.

So they were even. The girl knew how to fence.
Montalbano gestured towards the chair in front of his

desk, and she sat down, setting the large handbag she carried slung across her shoulder onto the floor.

She began speaking before the inspector had even asked her anything.

"My name is Roberta Rollo. We have the same rank, but for the past three years I've been in the direct employ of the UN."

So this must be a really big deal. And while she might be of equal rank to him, she certainly was far more important than a simple chief inspector of police. He wanted confirmation.

"Was it you who forced the commissioner to give the case back to me?"

"Not personally, no. But I pulled a few strings," she said, smiling.

"Could I ask you a few questions?"

"I'm indebted to you. Go right ahead."

"Was Shaikiri your informer on the *Vanna*?"

"Yes."

"And were you the person Shaikiri met at the carabinieri station?"

"Yes."

"The lieutenant told me it had something to do with terrorism, but I didn't believe it."

"That's not a question but an affirmation. But I'll answer anyway. You were right not to believe it."

"Because in fact it involved the illegal diamond trade."

She opened her eyes wide, and they became two little lakes the colour of the sky.

"How did you find that out so quickly? I was told you were a good policeman, but I had no idea you —"

"You're not too bad yourself, I must say. You got me to swallow whole your story about being the neglected niece of a rich yacht owner . . . Did you know that? You even managed to make me feel sorry for you. But then why, at the same time, did you indirectly provide me with a number of clues that would lead me to realize that you were a completely different person from the one you pretended to be?"

"I have no problem telling you the whole story. The morning we met, when you rescued me from an unexpected predicament, you introduced yourself as Inspector Montalbano, the very person I'd been told to contact, to enlist your cooperation on an operation that was to be launched shortly thereafter."

"And what was that?"

"We'd learned that Émile Lannec . . ."

Montalbano shook his head.

"What's wrong?"

"His name wasn't Lannec, but Jean-Pierre David."

The girl was astonished.

"So Lannec was David!"

"Did you know him?"

"I certainly did. But we didn't know they were the same person. How did you find that out?"

"I'll tell you later. Go on."

"At any rate, we'd learned that Lannec had left Paris to come here. And so —"

"What was Lannec's role?"

"Wait. He seemed to us to be a sort of troubleshooter. He would turn up whenever there were problems."

"And what was his role when he was David?"

"He was one of the leaders of the organization. A very important man. Then I got a message from Shaikiri saying that due to the bad weather the *Vanna* was heading for Vigàta. As you've probably already surmised, the *Vanna* and the *Ace of Hearts* belong to the same organization, though they have different responsibilities."

"And what are they?"

"The *Vanna* picks up the diamonds, and the *Ace of Hearts* sorts them out. Having them both at the same port, and knowing that Lannec was here too, presented us with a unique opportunity. Imagine if we'd known that Lannec was actually David! That was why I rushed to the scene. My intention was to see how things stood and then, if necessary, get you to organize a round-up. But there was one hitch. A big one. Those people know who I am, and they know I've been after them for some time . . . And as you've seen, they're people who won't hesitate to kill. So I planted a few doubts in your mind, in case something happened to me."

"I'd guessed as much. Then why did you disappear?"

"Because they suddenly found Lannec's body in the dinghy. I realized there would be a lot of commotion, and that it wouldn't work in my favour. And Lannec's murder, which must certainly have taken place on board the *Ace of Hearts*, changed the whole picture. I needed to think things over."

226

"I'm sorry, but what interest did the *Vanna* have in bringing Lannec's body back to land? If he was killed by their very own accomplices on the *Ace of Hearts* . . ."

"They didn't recognize him! They couldn't! They made a serious mistake by bringing him back to land! And, in fact, Shaikiri told me about a furious quarrel that had taken place between Giovannini and Sperlì on the one hand, and Zigami and Petit on the other . . . Do you know who they are?"

"Yes. The supposed owner of the *Ace of Hearts* and his secretary."

"And they were arguing precisely because the *Vanna* had dragged the body back to port."

"Are all crew members on both ships implicated?"

"On the *Ace of Hearts*, yes; on the *Vanna*, only Alvarez knows what's going on."

And that was why La Giovannini made certain that Shaikiri wasn't killed on board her yacht.

"Why only Alvarez?"

"Alvarez is Angolan, not Spanish, as everyone thinks. Apparently he was the one who originally got the late Mr Giovannini interested in the diamond trade."

"I see. And Shaikiri?"

"An agent of ours who'd succeeded in infiltrating their group. Their suspicions were probably aroused when he got himself arrested twice in barely twenty-four hours. Do you know how they killed him?"

"Yes. First they stuck his head into a bucket full of water to make it look like he'd drowned, and then —"

"No," she interrupted. "It's true they did it to make it look like he'd drowned, but the main reason was to torture him. But it looks like he broke down and talked."

"I'm sorry, but could you explain to me exactly what the UN has to do with all this?"

"Have you ever heard of the Kimberley Process?"

"Yes, but I still haven't had time to —"

"I'll sum it up for you in a few words. It's an international organization that was set up in 2002 to oversee the export and import of diamonds. So far the governments of sixty-nine different countries have agreed to comply with it. But, as you probably can imagine, some three or four per cent of all diamonds extracted are still done clandestinely."

"I see. But where does the UN come in?"

"The UN's role is to make sure the diamonds on the illegal circuit don't become blood diamonds."

Blood diamonds? What on earth could that mean? The young woman noticed his puzzlement.

"By that I mean diamonds that come illicitly from areas controlled by forces opposed to legitimate governments — guerrilla forces, rebels, tribal or political factions, adversaries of any kind . . . With the proceeds they can buy all the weapons they like."

"And what sort of situation are we dealing with here and now, in your opinion?"

"Well, I think we've been presented with an incredible opportunity, perhaps a unique one."

"Why do you say that?"

"The *Ace of Hearts*, which must certainly have a cargo of diamonds on board, has been stuck in your port with engine trouble. I am sure they summoned Lannec to pass him the diamonds, probably so he could take them back to Paris. But then Lannec got killed."

"Why, in your opinion?"

"I think Zigami will tell us that after we've arrested him."

"Any hypotheses?"

"I think Zigami has only been following orders. After the murder, I requested some more information from people who know more than I do. Apparently other elements at the top of the organization no longer had much confidence in him. Or it might have been some sort of internal struggle, I don't know. So the present situation is as follows. The diamonds are still on board the *Ace of Hearts*. Not only that, but there must also be some on board the *Vanna*, since the cruiser was unable to meet them out on the open sea to effect a transfer. I think they're desperately looking for someone to get them out of this fix."

Montalbano suddenly had an idea so outlandish that he gave a start in his chair.

"What's wrong?"

"I think they've already found their man."

"Who?"

"His name is Mimì Augello. He's my second-in-command."

The young woman seemed completely bewildered.

"He managed to infiltrate their group? How did he do that?"

"He has . . . let's just say he's endowed with . . . well, he has some extraordinary qualities."

"In what sense?"

Montalbano preferred to change the subject.

"First explain to me what you want to do."

"Fine, but then you must bring me up to date on your investigation."

"All right."

"What I want to do is rather simple: I've already managed to get search warrants for both boats. I've already spoken to the local commander of the Customs Police, and if they find diamonds, they'll arrest them all, with your help. And this has to be done by this evening. Otherwise we risk having them leave the port tonight or early tomorrow morning."

"There is one problem," said Montalbano. "What if the people on the *Ace of Hearts* notice too much activity on the quay, get suspicious, and head out to sea? That boat's got some powerful engines, and it's unlikely one of our boats could keep up with it."

"You're right. What do you suggest?"

"That we make it impossible for them to leave the port."

"How?"

"We put two of the Harbour Office's patrol vessels at the mouth of the harbour. They're armed and wouldn't have any problem blockading the cruiser."

"Will you see to that, or should I?"

"I think it's better for you to go and make the arrangements with the Harbour Office. You have more authority."

"All right. Now tell me about your second-in-command."

"He succeeded in infiltrating the *Vanna* with the help of someone from the Harbour Office, Lieutenant Belladonna, who introduced him to the *Vanna* as a representative of the wholesaler that furnishes the fuel."

Roberta Rollo screwed up her face.

"Sounds a little flimsy to me."

"Wait. The excuse was that the fuel they'd bought to restock was defective and contained sediment that could damage the engines. And so my man took samples from their tanks for examination. And in the meantime he's made friends with La Giovannini."

"What kind of friends?"

"Intimate. And he's led her to believe that he's the kind of person who's willing to do anything to make money. Giovannini has asked him to work for her."

"Where?"

"First in South Africa, and then in Sierra Leone."

"Sierra Leone has been and continues to be a nerve centre of the illegal diamond trade. And what did your man do?"

"He accepted."

"And is he going to leave with them?!" the young woman asked, alarmed.

"He wouldn't dream of it! This afternoon, at five, he has one last meeting with Giovannini and Sperli, during which he's going to try to extract as much information as possible."

The girl sat silent for a moment, then said:

"Maybe it's better to wait and hear what he has to say, before taking action."

"I agree."

"And how's your man going to get out of there?"

"He's going to get arrested. By me. The way Shaikiri did for you."

Roberta Rollo started laughing.

"Sounds like a good idea." She stood up. "All right, then we'll meet back up here around four," she continued. "I'm going to go to the Harbour Office and talk to the commander, and then back to the Customs Police to work out a few details."

Montalbano envied her eyes, which would get to see Laura.

Once she had left, he called Fazio in.

"Have a seat."

Then he noticed that Fazio was wearing a face fit for the Day of the Dead.

"What's wrong?" he asked.

"When you said we might have to arrest Inspector Augello, were you joking?"

"No."

"Why, then? What's he done? Look, it's not as if Augello and I are all that fond of each other, but I don't think he's the kind of person who —"

"We have to arrest him for his own good."

Fazio threw up his hands, resigned.

"Where?"

"At the port. And you have to make as much noise as possible."

"But can't you arrest him yourself? Here at the station? Without creating a sensation? Whatever he may have done, the man doesn't deserve —"

"If you would just let me speak, I'll tell you why and how we have to arrest him."

Mimì Augello came back out onto the deck of the *Vanna* just after six o'clock, accompanied by Captain Sperlì. Mimì came down the ladder; the captain remained on board.

The moment he set foot on the quay, Mimì pulled his handkerchief out of his pocket and blew his nose. Then he started walking towards his car.

He'd taken barely three steps when a police car, siren blaring, cut off his path with tyres screeching loudly. In a flash he sprang forward, circled round it, and started running madly towards the northern entrance of the port.

Meanwhile Fazio and Gallo got out of the car, pistols in hand, and started giving chase.

"Stop! Police!" Fazio cried.

And since Mimì kept running without paying any notice, Fazio fired a shot in the air. Mimì ran on.

As soon as Mimì came within range, the Customs Police officer standing guard at the northern entrance pointed his rifle at him.

"Stop or I'll shoot!" the man shouted.

Augello got scared.

For all he knew, he might very well shoot in earnest, unaware that the whole thing was staged. He suddenly stopped and put up his hands.

"Couldn't you have run a little less fast, Inspector?" a panting Fazio asked as he slapped the handcuffs on him.

Flanked by Fazio and Gallo, Augello retraced his steps back to the police car. The entire crew of the *Ace of Hearts*, having heard the shot and the shouting, were now out on the deck, watching him walk past. On the *Vanna*, there were instead only two spectators: Giovannini and Sperlì. But they were enough.

"*Matre santa!*" Mimì said, out of breath, to Montalbano, who had stayed in the car. "That Customs cop scared the life out of me!"

Back at the office, Inspector Rollo was already waiting for them. Montalbano introduced her to Augello and Fazio and explained who she was.

Mimì then turned to Montalbano.

"But, earlier today, did you come on board the *Vanna*?"

"Yes. I wanted to make them a little nervous, so that when you arrived around five, they —"

"Well, you certainly succeeded! Talk about nervous! Livia . . ."

It had slipped out. He stopped in midsentence, blushed, and looked at Roberta Rollo, who smiled amicably.

"Don't worry about it," said Montalbano.

"At a certain point, La Giovannini told Sperlì she was positive you'd worked everything out and that they

234

mustn't allow you any time to act. But what did you say to him?"

"I didn't say anything. I just let him notice, as if by chance, that I had some printouts on the Kimberley Process, which you'd mentioned to me, in my pocket. And so it must have looked to them as if I knew more about it than I actually do ... But tell me what happened."

"Well, as soon as I got there, La Giovannini was already very upset and told me she had changed her mind."

"They'd decided not to take you on?"

"No, they'd changed my function, but only temporarily."

"In what sense?"

"I was to carry a suitcase to Paris, taking an itinerary that they were going to explain to me tonight, shortly before they left. They plan to set sail at dawn. Then, after handing over the suitcase, I was to take a flight to Sierra Leone."

"And what did you say?"

"I said OK."

"What excuse did you use for leaving the ship?"

"I said I had to go to the police station to get my passport before the office closed at six."

"Did they specify that it was actually a suitcase and not an overnight bag?" Rollo asked.

"Yes. It was a rather large and heavy suitcase whose contents I was supposed to transfer later to two smaller suitcases."

Inspector Rollo whistled through clenched teeth.

"Apparently they put all the diamonds that were on both boats into a single suitcase. And they were going to get Inspector Augello to do what Lannec was supposed to have done. That much is clear. However . . . They were entrusting him with a cargo of immense value . . . a suitcase full of uncut diamonds . . . with no guarantee. Seems strange to me."

"Just a minute," said Mimì. "Giovannini told me I was going to leave for Paris late tomorrow morning. A car would come and pick me up, with another person besides the driver."

"So you were going to go all the way to Paris by car?"

"Yes."

"So, to conclude," said Inspector Rollo, "we know for certain that the diamonds are still on board. We must take immediate action."

She looked at her watch. It was a quarter to seven. "Now let me tell you what we're going to do."

CHAPTER
EIGHTEEN

At eight o'clock sharp, when there was still enough light, a Harbour Office car was going to stop in front of the *Ace of Hearts'* ladder, and an officer, on some pretext or other, would go on board to see how many crew members were present and then relay this information to Inspector Rollo via his mobile phone.

Rollo, meanwhile, would direct the operation from a car parked on the quay, far enough not to be seen but close enough so she could see everything. The information the officer would give her would be very important, because the crew of the *Ace of Hearts* had already killed at least two people and were criminals capable of anything. There was no need to do the same with the *Vanna*, since there were only three people implicated in the illegal traffic: Giovannini, Captain Sperli, and old Alvarez.

Rollo, in turn, would then communicate the number of people on board to Montalbano, who would be in the first of the two Vigàta police cars, driven by Gallo. The first as well as the second car — the latter directed by Fazio — would each have four policemen inside.

The two cars were then supposed to drive into the port through the northern entrance at high speed but

237

without sirens. The first would pull up in front of the *Ace of Hearts*, the second in front of the *Vanna*. The men would then pour out of the cars, weapons in hand, climb on board in every way possible, like pirates, and take control of the two boats.

The greater the element of surprise, the better.

The more difficult task would fall to the first car, since they would have to deal with the crew of the cruiser and would likely encounter some resistance.

Once everyone on board the two boats was immobilized, Rollo would call the Customs Police, who would already be waiting at the northern entrance, and tell them to search for the large suitcase with the uncut diamonds.

Not knowing how things would really play out, however, Montalbano had arranged for Mimì Augello to go with two men to all the bars and tavernas in Vigàta and arrest any sailor from the *Vanna* or *Ace of Hearts* that they encountered. All of them, even those who Inspector Rollo said had nothing to do with the plot. It was best to play it safe.

On paper, everything looked as if it should work out to perfection.

But with each minute that passed and brought him closer to the start, Montalbano felt a great sense of agitation growing inside him. And, without knowing why, he fidgeted and fretted inside the car, huffing as if he couldn't breathe.

There were four of them: Gallo beside him, and in the back, Galluzzo and Martorana, an alert young officer. The inspector had his pistol in his pocket, while the other three were armed with sub-machine guns.

238

Gallo kept the engine idling, ready to break into a Formula One dash.

Montalbano opened the car door.

"What, you want to get out?" a flummoxed Gallo asked him.

"No. I just want to smoke a cigarette."

"Then it'd be better if you shut the door and opened the window. If I have to suddenly take off . . ."

"OK, OK," the inspector said, forgoing the cigarette.

At that moment his phone rang.

"Lieutenant Belladonna has just gone on board the *Ace of Hearts*," Roberta Rollo told him.

Laura! *Matre santa*, it had never occurred to him they would stick her in the middle of this!

Why her, of all people?

"What did she say?" Gallo asked.

And what if the thugs reacted violently? What if they hurt her? What if —

"What did she say?" Gallo persisted.

"She said . . . La . . . La . . . she said Lalala . . . has boarded. What the fuck! What a stupid fucking idea!"

The inspector seemed so enraged that Gallo decided to let it drop, not daring to ask any more questions.

How on earth could they send a girl like Laura to carry out so dangerous an assignment? Were they crazy?

The phone rang again.

"There are five on board, two at the engines, and three on deck, but the lieutenant —"

Montalbano didn't wait to hear any more.

"Go!" he shouted.

He yelled it so loudly that his voice made his own ears ring along with those of the other three in the car. As Gallo shot off like a rocket, he looked in the mirror: Fazio's car was right behind, practically stuck to his bumper.

Rollo had calculated that they would need less than four minutes to get from the northern entrance to the *Ace of Hearts*, but Gallo had laughed at this, saying he could get there in less than half the time. But Rollo had also decided that to avoid arousing suspicion, the normal traffic in the port should be allowed to continue.

As a result, no sooner did Montalbano's car fly out from the alleyway in which it was hidden and come to the north entrance, than it found its path blocked by an HGV.

The driver was out of the cab, showing his card to the Customs guard.

Montalbano was blind with terror and rage.

In the twinkling of an eye, and cursing all the while, he opened the door, jumped out, and, taking the pedestrian crossing, started running towards the *Ace of Hearts*.

And at once he saw, in the distance, something he wished he hadn't seen.

One of the sailors on the cruiser had just lifted the mooring hawser from the bollard and was climbing back on board. And was the dull, incessant thumping he heard his own blood or was it the rumble of the *Ace of Hearts'* powerful engines?

He sped up as much as he could, feeling a sharp pain in his side.

Without knowing how he got there, he found himself at the top of the ladder that had been left attached to the quay, with the deck of the cruiser at the same level as him but already a good two feet away. They were escaping.

He closed his eyes and jumped.

He realized he had his gun in his hand, though he couldn't remember when he had taken it out of his pocket. He was acting purely on instinct.

He landed on the stern, entirely out in the open. The first shot they fired from the cabin whizzed by his head. He reacted by firing two shots blindly, come what may, in the general direction of the wheelhouse, as he ran and hid behind a large coil of hawser that was pretty useless as a shield.

Then he realized he was very close to the hatch leading below.

He had to get there. They were still firing at him from the cabin, but as the cruiser rapidly gained speed, it danced about on the water, making it hard for them to take aim.

Then, after firing three rapid shots in a row, the inspector took another great leap and ended up rolling down the steps of the little ladder leading below.

As he picked himself up, he froze.

There before him, back against a wall, was Laura, staring at him in silence, eyes popping in terror.

What was she doing still on board?

For a moment he drowned in the blue of her eyes.

That brief moment sufficed to allow the man behind him to stick the barrel of a revolver into the middle of his back.

"Make a move and I'll kill you," said a voice with a slight French accent.

It must be Petit, Zigami's secretary. Who was not, however, aware of just how much desperate courage Laura's eyes had inspired in Montalbano.

Without his body showing the slightest sign of turning, the inspector's left foot rose as if by its own will with animal speed and forcefully, ferociously struck the Frenchman square in the balls, making him double over, groaning and dropping his weapon. Just to be sure, Montalbano dealt him another swift kick square in the face. Petit collapsed.

Then in a single bound Montalbano was beside Laura and pushed her by the shoulders as far as the little ladder. He bent down and grabbed the Frenchman's pistol. Now he could fire away without needing to save any shots.

"I'm going to go up to the top of the stairs and start firing at the wheelhouse. When you hear the first shot, run across the deck and jump into the water. But from the side of the boat, to avoid the propellers. Got that?"

She nodded yes. Then, making a great effort to speak, she asked:

"What about you?"

"I'll jump in after you. Here I go."

But then she laid her hand on his arm. And Montalbano understood. He leaned forward and kissed her, ever so lightly, on the lips.

He crawled up the six steps and started firing. Laura streaked by him and disappeared. But they were returning his fire from the cabin and there wasn't a second to lose.

He stood up and, jumping like a kangaroo across the deck, reached the side, stepped over it, and plunged into the water.

At once he realized that Laura was nowhere in sight. At the high speed the cruiser had reached, the few seconds between one jump and the next had put a great distance between them.

On top of everything else, night had fallen. Taking his bearings, however, from the lights he could see in the distance, he realized he was right in the middle of the harbour.

Letting go of the guns, which he no longer needed, he took off his jacket and shoes and started swimming against the foaming wake the cruiser had left behind.

He called out loudly:

"Laura! Laura!"

Silence. Why didn't she answer? Maybe her violent landing in the water had temporarily deafened her?

He was about to call out to her again when all at once, at the mouth of the harbour, there was a tremendous burst of automatic weapons' fire. It sounded like a veritable naval battle. Apparently the cruiser was trying to force its way through the Coast Guard's blockade and reach the open sea.

Then there was a tremendous explosion and the water all around turned red, reflecting the flames of a great fire.

So much for the *Ace of Hearts*, he thought. Perhaps it had been hit in the fuel tanks.

And it was by the continually changing light of that blaze, which made the water look as if it might itself turn to flame, that Montalbano spotted Laura's body floating, about twenty yards away, moved only by the gentle rippling of the sea.

"Oh my God, my God . . . Oh please, God . . ."

Was he praying? He didn't know, but if he was indeed praying, it was for the first time in his life.

He swam over to her. She was floating on her back, eyes open as if watching the night's first stars, and barely breathing, her mouth wide open.

She didn't even realize that Montalbano was beside her and holding her head above the water with his arm under her shoulders.

With that same hand he touched the terrible wound that had rent Laura's flesh.

They must have hit her as she was jumping into the sea.

But the important thing was that she was still breathing, and so he had to bring her to shore immediately.

He went underwater, swam under her body, then resurfaced.

Now they were shoulder to shoulder, and Montalbano held her tightly against him with his left arm and started swimming with his free arm and his feet.

After less than five minutes of this, a searchlight spotted them, and at once a motorboat was rumbling beside him, motor idling low, and Fazio's voice called out.

"You can let her go, Chief. We'll get the lieutenant ourselves."

★ ★ ★

Later, at the station, he changed into the clothes and shoes that Gallo had gone to fetch for him in Marinella. And he'd already guzzled half of the bottle of whisky that he'd had Catarella buy for him, before Roberta Rollo came in, happy and triumphant.

Congratulations, Inspector. Thanks to your courage . . .
   Everyone on the *Ace of Hearts* died in the explosion.
   Why hadn't they let him get into the ambulance with Laura?

The suitcase with the uncut diamonds was recovered by the Customs Police. Livia Giovannini, Captain Sperli, and Maurilio Alvarez have been arrested.
   Was she suffering a lot? Would they manage to save her?

We have delivered a very harsh blow to the illegal blood-diamonds trade. They won't easily recover from it.
   I intend to highlight your invaluable contribution, Inspector, in my report to the United Nations.
   She'd wanted him to kiss her. Perhaps she had a premonition of what was about to happen to her?

Tomorrow we're going to hold a press conference here, at the police station.
   The look she'd given him when he suddenly appeared on the *Ace of Hearts!*

Things really couldn't have gone any better than this.
   Really? No better? No better for who?

By the time he left the station it was past midnight.

For all those hours he had opened his mouth barely three or four times, to answer questions. And Fazio must have noticed that there was something out of kilter with him, because he kept looking over at him.

For his own part, the inspector had asked only two questions, both for Roberta Rollo.

"But did you know that Lieutenant Belladonna was still on board the *Ace of Hearts?*"

"Of course! I even told you!"

It was true. Now he remembered. Rollo had started saying, "But the lieutenant . . ." but he hadn't let her finish the sentence.

His second question was:

"And would you have had them fire at the cruiser even if you'd known the lieutenant was on board?"

"No, in fact I immediately told the Coast Guard not to open fire, even if this meant losing the game. But you took care of that. As soon as I saw you both jump into the water, I told them they could fire away."

No, he couldn't go home to Marinella without news of Laura. He got in his car and headed for Montelusa.

At that hour one wasn't allowed to enter the hospital, but perhaps someone in accident and emergency could tell him something.

As soon as he went in, however, he realized it was hopeless. A bus full of tourists had fallen into a ravine and there were some thirty-odd injured who urgently needed care.

He left demoralized. As he was about to head to the car park where he'd left the car, he heard someone call him. Turning around, he saw that it was Mario Scala, an inspector from the Anti-Mafia Commission.

"Hey, Salvo. I just heard a little while ago at the office about your heroic actions. Congratulations. What are you doing here?"

"I wanted to know if there was any news about a lieutenant from the Harbour Office, named Belladonna, a young woman who . . ."

His throat went dry and he couldn't go on. He managed only to ask:

"And how about you?"

"I've got a Mafia turncoat here, a state's witness who's registered at the hospital under a false name. But I still worry about him, so I come and see him from time to time . . . What did you say the lieutenant's name was?"

"Belladonna?"

"Wait here."

He returned some ten minutes later after Montalbano had chain-smoked five cigarettes.

Mario Scala had a very serious expression on his face.

"They performed emergency surgery. It was a miracle she even made it to the hospital alive. She'd lost too much blood. She's on life support now."

"Is she going to make it?"

"They're hoping. But she's in a very grave condition."

★   ★   ★

Since the car park was almost entirely deserted, the inspector got into his car, turned on the ignition, and pulled the vehicle round to have a good view of the main entrance. There were two unopened packs of cigarettes in the glove compartment.

He could spend the whole night there. And he did.

Every so often he got out of the car, walked around, looked up at the hospital's facade, and then got back into the car.

Then, at dawn's first, violet light, he saw a man in uniform come out of the front door and immediately start talking on his mobile phone.

It was Lieutenant Garrufo!

Montalbano jumped out of the car, ran up to the lieutenant, and brusquely pulled the arm holding the phone away from the man's face.

"How is Laura?" he asked.

Garrufo was about to get angry but luckily recognized him at once.

"Ah, it's you. Just a second."

He brought the mobile phone back to his ear.

"I'll call you back later."

"How is she?" Montalbano asked again.

Garrufo's uniform was all rumpled and he looked as if he hadn't slept a wink all night.

He threw up his hands, and Montalbano felt sick at heart.

"I don't know what to say, Inspector. She's pretty far gone. I spent the whole night at her side, and when they took her to the operating room I waited outside, in the corridor. Right before the operation she had a moment of lucidity, but then nothing."

"Did she manage to say anything?"

And here it seemed to Montalbano that the lieutenant had suddenly felt a little embarrassed.

"Yes. She repeated a name twice." He paused a moment, and then asked: "Your first name is Salvo, isn't it?"

The tone he used made this a statement, not a question. Silence fell over them. Then Garrufo said:

"We've informed her fiancé. But he won't be able to come. He doesn't think he can ask for permission."

The dream in which Livia had refused to come to his funeral flashed through the inspector's mind. But what did that have to do with anything? What a thought! Perhaps the effect of sleep deprivation? That was a dream, and this was . . .

"The chief surgeon told me he found it very strange that Laura wasn't cooperating."

"Cooperating in what sense?"

"He said that, since she's such a young woman, her body should instinctively react and cooperate, even on the unconscious level. Whereas . . . Well, I guess I'll go back inside."

She didn't want to react, didn't want to cooperate to save herself, Montalbano thought as he walked towards his car with a lump in his throat and his heart as tight as a fist. Perhaps because she'd made a choice. Or more likely because she wanted to take herself out of the game, so she wouldn't have to make a choice.

He sat down in the car on the passenger's side.

An hour later, the door on the driver's side opened, and someone got in and sat down. He didn't turn to see who it was, because by this point he was unable to take his eyes off the hospital entrance.

"I went to Marinella to look for you," said Fazio, "but you weren't there. Then I realized you'd be here, and so I came."

Montalbano didn't answer.

Half an hour later, he saw Garrufo come out, bent over, face in his hands, weeping.

"Take me home," he said to Fazio.

He leaned his head back against the headrest and closed his eyes, at last.

Author's Note

The only thing in this novel connected to reality is the Kimberley Process. Everything else, from the characters' names to the situations in which they find themselves, is the fruit of my imagination.

Notes

page *13* — **a novel** . . . *The Solitude of Prime Numbers: La solitudine dei numeri primi,* by author and mathematician Paolo Giordano, 2008 (English translation by Shaun Whiteside, Penguin, 2009).

page *16* — **"honourables":** in Italy, members of parliament are called "honourables" (*onorevoli*).

page *16* — **the Cozzi — Pini law:** a thinly disguised reference to the Bossi — Fini law, drawn up by Umberto Bossi and Gianfranco Fini, leaders respectively of the xenophobic Northern League and the National Alliance, a right-wing party descended directly from the Neofascist MSI Party founded after the Second World War. Enacted in 2002 by the Italian parliament, with the ruling coalition of Silvio Berlusconi's Forza Italia Party and these two smaller parties holding an absolute majority, this heavy-handed law, among its many provisions, makes it illegal for individuals not belonging to EU member nations to enter the country without a work contract, requires all non-EU individuals who lose their jobs while in the country to repatriate to their country of origin, abolishes the sponsorship system that had previously enabled non-EU individuals to enter the country under the patronage of a sponsor already in Italy, establishes the government's right to decree a quota of the number of non-EU individuals allowed to enter the country over the period of one year, and makes all foreign nationals not in conformity with these new guidelines subject to criminal proceedings and/or forced repatriation.

page 20 — **"Garruso . . . Mebbe 'e's from up north"**: garruso is a common Sicilian insult, homophobic in nature but used generally to mean "jerk", "prick", "arsehole", etc. A literal translation would be more like "poof".

page 30 — **the *Settimana Enigmistica***: an immensely popular Italian weekly periodical of puzzles, such as rebuses, acrostics, crosswords, riddles, etc. Created in 1932, it is also published in a number of other European countries.

page 34 — **"Two months before Nasiriya"**: as part of George W. Bush's war on Iraq, launched in March 2003, Italy, under Silvio Berlusconi, the right-wing Prime Minister, committed three thousand soldiers to the effort, helping to form part of what was called the "Coalition of the Willing". The modern town of Nasiriya, an important petrol centre with a population of over 250,000, was severely damaged by American bombs and fighting during the war and became a centre for the small Italian contingent, who built a hospital there, among other things. On 12 November 2003, a suicide bombing by the Iraqi resistance killed twenty-three, including nineteen Italians, resulting in a fierce outcry among Italians at home, who had been overwhelmingly against the American declaration of war and Berlusconi's agreement to participate in an effort they believed unjust. By having the character of Vanna Digiulio killed in a secret operation before the Nasiriya bombing, Camilleri appears to be highlighting what he views as the murky nature of the Italian participation in an unjustifiable war.

page 40 — **Belladonna . . . The lieutenant not only lived up to her surname, she exceeded it:** in Italian, *"bella donna"* means "beautiful woman".

page 57 — *nervetti*: marinated veal shanks, often served as antipasto.

page 90 — **Umberto Saba . . .** *such was the way / of wisdom*: from the poem "Favoletta" in *Cuor Morituro* (1925–1930), translation from *Songbook: The Selected Poems of Umberto Saba*, translated by Stephen Sartarelli (Riverdale-on-Hudson: Sheep Meadow Press, 1998), p. 131.

page 110 — **seeing an enemy enter the camp of Agramante:** Agramante is one of the leaders of the Saracen knights in *Orlando Furioso*, the fanciful verse romance by Ludovico Ariosto (1474–1533) loosely based on the Carolingian cycle of medieval *chansons de geste*. Episodes from *Orlando Furioso* provide much of the material used in the *teatro dei pupi*, the traditional Sicilian puppet theatre one can still see in the streets of Sicily today.

page 138 — **the equestrienne:** see Andrea Camilleri, *The Track of Sand* (Picador, 2011).

page 204 — **once they got past the stumbling block of the K, there was still the Y at the end:** the Italian language contains neither the letter K nor the letter Y.

Notes by Stephen Sartarelli

Also available in ISIS Large Print:

The Bones of Avignon

Jefferson Bass

It's the discovery that will make Miranda Lovelady's career ... if she can prove it. The secret she's unearthed is enough to convince Dr Bill Brockton to abandon the Body Farm and fly to Avignon. The medieval city is picturesque, but deadly.

When their colleague is found crucified in a ruined chapel, Brockton and Miranda become entangled in a terrifying conspiracy, far bigger than either of them can imagine. Unearthing the bones of Jesus of Nazareth would be the find of the millennium. And when the secret leaks, there will be people watching: the Vatican, the police, and a murderous fanatic, who plans to use the bones to trigger the Apocalypse.

ISBN 978-0-7531-9148-4 (hb)
ISBN 978-0-7531-9149-1 (pb)

The Blind Goddess

Anne Holt

A drug dealer is battered to death on the outskirts of Oslo. A young Dutch student, covered in blood, walks aimlessly through the streets of the city. He is taken into custody, but refuses to speak. Five days later a shady criminal lawyer called Hansa Larsen is murdered. The two deaths don't seem related, but Detective Inspector Hanne Wilhelmsen is unconvinced. Soon, she uncovers a link between the bodies: Larsen defended the drug dealer.

But there are powerful forces working against Hanne; a conspiracy that reaches far beyond a crooked lawyer and a small-time dealer. The investigation will take her into the offices of the most powerful men in Norway — and even put her own life at risk . . .

ISBN 978-0-7531-9114-9 (hb)
ISBN 978-0-7531-9115-6 (pb)

Bitter Water

Gordon Ferris

Glasgow's melting. The temperature is rising and so is the murder rate. Douglas Brodie, ex-policeman, ex-soldier and newst reporter on the Glasgow Gazette, has no shortage of material for his crime column. But even Brodie balks at his latest subject — a rapist who has been tarred and feathered by a balaclava-clad group. Brodie soon discovers a link between this horrific act and a series of brutal beatings. As violence spreads and the bodies pile up, Brodie and advocate Samantha Campbell are entangled in a web of deception and savagery. Brodie is swamped with stories for the Gazette. But how long becore he and Sam become the headline?

ISBN 978-0-7531-9110-1 (hb)
ISBN 978-0-7531-9111-8 (pb)

The Death of a Mafia Don

Michele Giuttari

A bomb explodes in the centre of Florence, hitting the car of Chief Superintendent Michele Ferrara of the elite Squadra Mobile. The attack rocks the ancient city to its foundations. Ferrara was clearly the target — and he did, after all, just controversially imprison notorious Mafia boss Salvatore Laprua. A week later, another bomb explodes — bringing tragedy for Ferrara and a determination to find the culprit. But that same morning, Salvatore Laprua is found dead in his prison cell. So who is the mysterious influence behind the bombings — someone even the Mafia fear?

ISBN 978-0-7531-8788-3 (hb)
ISBN 978-0-7531-8789-0 (pb)